TO BELIEVE THE TRUTH
DI SAM COBBS A LAKE DISTRICT THRILLER
BOOK TWELVE

M A COMLEY

Copyright © 2024 by M A Comley

All rights reserved.

No part of this book may be reproduced in any form or by any electronic or mechanical means, including information storage and retrieval systems, without written permission from the author, except for the use of brief quotations in a book review.

Thank you once again to Clive Rowlandson for allowing me to use one of his stunning photos for the cover.

ALSO BY M A COMLEY

Blind Justice (Novella)
Cruel Justice (Book #1)
Mortal Justice (Novella)
Impeding Justice (Book #2)
Final Justice (Book #3)
Foul Justice (Book #4)
Guaranteed Justice (Book #5)
Ultimate Justice (Book #6)
Virtual Justice (Book #7)
Hostile Justice (Book #8)
Tortured Justice (Book #9)
Rough Justice (Book #10)
Dubious Justice (Book #11)
Calculated Justice (Book #12)
Twisted Justice (Book #13)
Justice at Christmas (Short Story)
Prime Justice (Book #14)
Heroic Justice (Book #15)
Shameful Justice (Book #16)
Immoral Justice (Book #17)
Toxic Justice (Book #18)
Overdue Justice (Book #19)
Unfair Justice (a 10,000 word short story)
Irrational Justice (a 10,000 word short story)

Seeking Justice (a 15,000 word novella)
Caring For Justice (a 24,000 word novella)
Savage Justice (a 17,000 word novella)
Justice at Christmas #2 (a 15,000 word novella)
Gone in Seconds (Justice Again series #1)
Ultimate Dilemma (Justice Again series #2)
Shot of Silence (Justice Again series #3)
Taste of Fury (Justice Again series #4)
Crying Shame (Justice Again series #5)
See No Evil (Justice Again #6)
To Die For (DI Sam Cobbs #1)
To Silence Them (DI Sam Cobbs #2)
To Make Them Pay (DI Sam Cobbs #3)
To Prove Fatal (DI Sam Cobbs #4)
To Condemn Them (DI Sam Cobbs #5)
To Punish Them (DI Sam Cobbs #6)
To Entice Them (DI Sam Cobbs #7)
To Control Them (DI Sam Cobbs #8)
To Endanger Lives (DI Sam Cobbs #9)
To Hold Responsible (DI Sam Cobbs #10)
To Catch a Killer (DI Sam Cobbs #11)
To Believe The Truth (DI Sam Cobbs #12)
To Blame Them (DI Sam Cobbs #13)
Forever Watching You (DI Miranda Carr thriller)
Wrong Place (DI Sally Parker thriller #1)
No Hiding Place (DI Sally Parker thriller #2)
Cold Case (DI Sally Parker thriller#3)
Deadly Encounter (DI Sally Parker thriller #4)

Lost Innocence (DI Sally Parker thriller #5)
Goodbye My Precious Child (DI Sally Parker #6)
The Missing Wife (DI Sally Parker #7)
Truth or Dare (DI Sally Parker #8)
Where Did She Go? (DI Sally Parker #9)
Sinner (DI Sally Parker #10)
The Good Die Young (DI Sally Parker #11)
Coping Without You (DI Sally Parker #12)
Web of Deceit (DI Sally Parker Novella)
The Missing Children (DI Kayli Bright #1)
Killer On The Run (DI Kayli Bright #2)
Hidden Agenda (DI Kayli Bright #3)
Murderous Betrayal (Kayli Bright #4)
Dying Breath (Kayli Bright #5)
Taken (DI Kayli Bright #6)
The Hostage Takers (DI Kayli Bright Novella)
No Right to Kill (DI Sara Ramsey #1)
Killer Blow (DI Sara Ramsey #2)
The Dead Can't Speak (DI Sara Ramsey #3)
Deluded (DI Sara Ramsey #4)
The Murder Pact (DI Sara Ramsey #5)
Twisted Revenge (DI Sara Ramsey #6)
The Lies She Told (DI Sara Ramsey #7)
For The Love Of… (DI Sara Ramsey #8)
Run for Your Life (DI Sara Ramsey #9)
Cold Mercy (DI Sara Ramsey #10)
Sign of Evil (DI Sara Ramsey #11)
Indefensible (DI Sara Ramsey #12)

Locked Away (DI Sara Ramsey #13)

I Can See You (DI Sara Ramsey #14)

The Kill List (DI Sara Ramsey #15)

Crossing The Line (DI Sara Ramsey #16)

Time to Kill (DI Sara Ramsey #17)

Deadly Passion (DI Sara Ramsey #18)

Son Of The Dead (DI Sara Ramsey #19)

Evil Intent (DI Sara Ramsey #20)

The Games People Play (DI Sara Ramsey #21)

Revenge Streak (DI Sara Ramsey #22)

Seeking Retribution (DI Sara Ramsey #23)

I Know The Truth (A Psychological thriller)

She's Gone (A psychological thriller)

Shattered Lives (A psychological thriller)

Evil In Disguise – a novel based on True events

Deadly Act (Hero series novella)

Torn Apart (Hero series #1)

End Result (Hero series #2)

In Plain Sight (Hero Series #3)

Double Jeopardy (Hero Series #4)

Criminal Actions (Hero Series #5)

Regrets Mean Nothing (Hero series #6)

Prowlers (Hero Series #7)

Sole Intention (Intention series #1)

Grave Intention (Intention series #2)

Devious Intention (Intention #3)

Cozy mysteries

Murder at the Wedding

Murder at the Hotel

Murder by the Sea

Death on the Coast

Death By Association

Merry Widow (A Lorne Simpkins short story)

It's A Dog's Life (A Lorne Simpkins short story)

A Time To Heal (A Sweet Romance)

A Time For Change (A Sweet Romance)

High Spirits

The Temptation series (Romantic Suspense/New Adult Novellas)

Past Temptation

Lost Temptation

Clever Deception (co-written by Linda S Prather)

Tragic Deception (co-written by Linda S Prather)

Sinful Deception (co-written by Linda S Prather)

ACKNOWLEDGMENTS

Special thanks as always go to @studioenp for their superb cover design expertise.

My heartfelt thanks go to my wonderful editor Emmy, and my proofreaders Joseph and Barbara for spotting all the lingering nits.

Thank you also to my amazing ARC Group who help to keep me sane during this process.

RIP Mum, you've taken a huge part of my heart with you. Until we meet again.

To Mary, gone, but never forgotten. I hope you found the peace you were searching for my dear friend. I miss you each and every day.

PROLOGUE

Alvin hated venturing out at night. Being a farmer, he regarded himself as a morning person. That's where he felt more at home, rounding up the cows for milking and feeding the pigs. Being out in the wide open like this stretched him to his limits and pushed him way out of his comfort zone.

"I need to get going now, Fred. I told Bethany that I wouldn't be long. That was a couple of hours ago."

"You're under the thumb, that's your problem. I wouldn't allow no bloody woman to dictate what I do and when I do it. Sod that for a game of soldiers."

Alvin laughed and shook his head. He jumped off the bar stool and leaned in. "That's why you're thrice divorced and spend every night, rain or shine, down the pub with this mob."

"'Ere, I dispute that," his old farming chum slurred. "It's not every night. And before you start, these are my friends, our friends. Who you appear to have neglected lately, or had you forgotten that?"

"Nope, you know what I'm like about going out at night,

especially during the winter when the nights are darker and miserable. I'd much rather be at home, feet up in front of the open fire."

"Ha, who are you trying to kid? You mean at her beck and call all the time."

"You know nothing about our marriage, so keep your opinions to yourself, old-timer. I'm off. My aim, this evening, was to pop in here for a quick one on the way home. Mission accomplished. Now I can hear a chicken casserole calling my name."

"Cluck, cluck. Are you sure it's not that Mother Hen of yours?"

The rest of the crowd laughed at Fred's quip.

"I'm sure. Enjoy the rest of your evening, folks." Alvin waved farewell with a smile fixed in place.

He detested them all laughing at him and shuddered at the thought of what the rest of their evening would entail, them running him down behind his back. Shrugging, he got in the car and headed out of town, towards the farm. He didn't get far when the car began kangaroo jumping before it finally stuttered to a halt. He lashed out at the steering wheel and pulled the lever to open the bonnet. The road was quiet, now that the rush hour had died down and, with no houses close by on this stretch of his journey, there was no one around to give him a hand.

After removing the torch from the passenger door, he raised the bonnet and secured it in place while he had a quick gander. He'd ditched his breakdown service when the cost had doubled since last year and now, here he was, regretting that idiotic decision. He tweaked a few wires, ensured everything was in place or where it should be, then lowered the bonnet again.

He turned the key in the ignition and nothing, still as dead as the area surrounding him. He went back and took a closer peek under the bonnet. Not that he had any idea what he was looking for, he lacked the skills to know how a car worked. Topping up with diesel and oil now and again and maybe changing the odd spark plug was as good as it got in that respect.

Again, as far as he could tell, there was nothing out of place. A noise sounded behind him. Before he had a chance to sneak a glance over his shoulder, someone clouted him over the head. His legs gave way beneath him, but the person caught him, prevented him from falling. Dazed, he peered through the darkness at his attacker, but his focus remained blurred.

"What are you doing? Who are you?" he whispered.

"Get in the car." The tone was abrupt, stern even.

Alvin staggered back to the driver's seat with the assailant's help. Another whack to the head, and he lost consciousness.

HE WASN'T sure how long he was out cold for but, when he woke up, he was choking on fumes, and the heat surrounding him was intense.

His head, still thumping from the whacks he'd received, crushed his ability to come up with a plan of action to get him out of the fix he'd found himself in. He coughed, his eyes stinging from the fumes. He knew he had to get out of the vehicle before the flames consumed it, and him. But then the car exploded…

CHAPTER 1

Sam's phone vibrated on the bedside table close to her head. Luckily, she was a light sleeper and stopped it before it disturbed Rhys. She tiptoed across the room and closed the door to the en suite then answered the phone.

"DI Sam Cobbs. This better be good at this hour of the morning."

"Umm… sorry to trouble you, ma'am. I've been asked to call you by the pathologist on our patch."

"So what's new? And? Why?"

"Because he's requesting your attendance at a scene."

"Jesus. Okay, I should have guessed it would be something like that. You'd better give me the details. On second thoughts, I haven't got a pen or paper handy, and I don't want to disturb my fiancé who is still lost somewhere, deep in the land of nod."

"I can text you the information when I'm finished, how's that?"

"It'll have to do. You're going to have to give my partner a call as well. Why should I be the only one who loses out on sleep around here?"

The woman laughed. "I can action that, too, ma'am. Your presence is required at the industrial estate out at Stainburn."

"I think I know the one. What's the crime?"

"A car has exploded, or it did last night, at around seven."

"I'm listening. How does this concern me?"

"The pathologist believes the incident is a suspicious one, that's as much as I know. Sorry, ma'am."

"Okay. Well, it's a good job I trust my pathologist friend. I know he wouldn't call me unless it was urgent. I'll get dressed and be on the road in ten minutes, if you can let the pathologist know. It'll save me having to fend off his calls every five minutes. I know what an impatient bugger he can be at times."

"I'll do that now, Inspector. Thank you for taking my call and being prepared to attend the scene."

"You're welcome. Not the best way to start a day, but it's not the first time I've uttered those words over the years, and I doubt if it will be the last."

"Yes, ma'am. Have a good day."

Sam smiled and shook her head. "You might want to rephrase that."

"Ah, yes. Sorry, ma'am."

"Speak soon, no doubt." Sam ended the call and ran the shower. She avoided wetting her hair, swiftly washed all over and quickly cleaned her teeth. She thought about what she was going to wear for the day and set about collecting what she needed and entered the bedroom.

Rhys was still snoring gently. She kissed him on the cheek. Casper and Sonny lifted their heads and wagged their tails from their comfy beds on the other side of the room. She gathered her clothes and snuck downstairs. She despised getting dressed without the heating going on and struggled to stop her teeth from chattering, but she didn't have an option this morning.

She glanced at the clock in the kitchen—five-thirty. She couldn't remember the last time she'd seen this ungodly hour, let alone been called into action to start her day. Her eyes rose to the ceiling. "I hope you're watching over me, Mum. I miss you every minute of the day." The words had become her daily mantra since the passing of her mother three months ago.

Sam dashed into the hallway and slipped on her black ankle boots then hitched into her black woollen coat which she fastened, hoping it would warm her up.

"Running out on me, are you?" Rhys called out from the top of the stairs, startling her.

"Jesus, give a girl some kind of warning before you frighten the shit out of her."

"Sorry. Have you had a call?"

"Believe me, do you really think I'd be venturing out there on a nippy January morning if I hadn't? Go back to bed, it's far too cold for you to be standing there naked, as much as I'm admiring the view."

"Oops, I didn't even think about it." He glanced down at his manhood and chuckled. "That explains the lack of excitement this morning, the chill in the air."

Sam laughed. "Likely story."

She ran up the stairs. He met her a few steps from the top, and they shared a kiss. Neither of the dogs had appeared. They had more sense than to leave their warm beds at this time of the morning.

"I've got to fly. I'll give you a call later. Love you."

He smiled. "Love you more. Take care on the roads, Sam, watch out for any icy spots."

"I will, thanks for caring."

"Always," he shouted after her.

The biting wind did its best to push her towards the car. As she turned to face it, her cheeks froze. Winter was truly here now. There had been warnings that snow was imminent, but it was still too dark for her to make out if any snow had settled on the hills overnight or not. No doubt that would become apparent later at sunrise. She searched for the pair of woollen mittens she kept in her glove box to combat the cold steering wheel and switched on the engine. It would take her at least fifteen minutes to get to the scene, more if the roads turned out to be treacherous. Hopefully, the gritters would have been out during the night.

In the end, the drive turned out to be an uneventful one. Bob was already at the scene. He was talking to Des. They were both stamping their feet and rubbing their hands to keep warm.

"Nice of you to finally show up," Des said.

"What a bloody cheek. Some of us have a life to lead. I was tucked up in bed, snuggled under the quilt with…"

Des raised a hand to prevent her from completing her sentence. "That's too much information. I've been here since three. I was just telling your partner here, that I feel like my nuts have dropped off in this cold weather."

"Umm… now that's too much information if ever I heard it."

"Shall we get on?" Des replied sharpish.

"Why not? Do we need to get suited up?"

"Always. Make it snappy before the smaller parts of my anatomy begin to drop off."

Sam rushed back to the boot of her car, slipped on a suit and removed a pair of covers that she would place over her boots once she got closer to the scene.

"How many people inside the vehicle?" she asked.

Des led the way back to the scene with Sam and Bob in hot pursuit, their suits rustling.

"One. Don't ask me if the victim is male or female, it's impossible to tell at the moment, in this light and given the condition the body is in."

"Crap. Why are we here? By that I mean, why do you think the incident is suspicious?"

"That's easy. One of the techs found a rag of sorts shoved up the exhaust pipe that would have caused the car to malfunction. My take is he probably stopped to see what the problem was. The bonnet was up, and he was sitting in the car. Maybe he was testing it, turned the engine over, and the car unexpectedly burst into flames."

"From a rag being shoved up the exhaust pipe? I've not come across that before."

"It depends on what the car had on board. How much fuel was in the tank," Bob suggested.

"That's very true," Des agreed. "I see we're on the same wavelength… finally, Sergeant, it's taken a while."

Bob rolled his eyes at Sam. She suppressed a giggle, used to Des' sharp tongue at the scene of a crime, if anyone dared to state the obvious.

"Is there a plate we can run through the system?" Sam asked the most obvious question she could think of.

"A partial one. It melted and dropped off the car. One of the techs found it a little while ago."

"Bob, can you note down the details and we'll run it through the system ASAP?"

"See Mitch, over the back there," Des advised.

He pointed at the tech he had mentioned, and Bob made his way towards the man.

"What's the background to the incident?" Sam asked. "I was told it happened at around seven, is that right?"

"Correct. A passing motorist saw the car on fire and

called the brigade. I've got his details here." He handed Sam a sheet of paper with an address.

"Thanks, we'll check in with him later. Why the delay in calling us?"

"I had a family wiped out in a car on the motorway to contend with, hence me not arriving until a few hours ago. And yes, that means I haven't slept in over thirty-six hours or more. To tell you the truth, I've lost count."

"Jesus, Des, you still need your sleep, everyone does. That's how mistakes happen."

He cocked an eyebrow. "Not on my watch, it doesn't. I know I could have shoved the bodies in the fridge and attended the scene sooner, but you know me, I believe in dealing with PMs when they're needed, not when they're convenient to what's going on around me."

"I know, you're a perfectionist. And now you have another post-mortem on your hands to deal with."

Des shrugged. "That's the nature of the job."

"When do you reckon you'll be able to get the victim out of the car?"

"How long's that piece of string in your pocket, Inspector? We're doing everything else that is needed for an investigation first. The car was still smoking when we got here. In answer to your question, we should be shifting the body soon."

Bob rejoined them. "The guys back at the station are running the plate through the system now, trying to match it to the vehicle."

"I bet that will take a while." Sam scanned the area. The nearest house was somewhere out there, off in the distance. "We're up shit creek until we've got more to go on. Let's have a mooch around, see if we can find any clues."

"I wouldn't bother," Des pitched in. "My guys have been

checking the area thoroughly for hours now, no clues found so far."

Sam kicked out at a nearby stone. "Shit, we're going to need to do something to keep ourselves warm out here."

"I could start another fire," Bob said.

Sam scowled at him. "Not funny, partner."

"Sorry, I'm still half asleep. What do you suggest we do then?"

Sam glared at him long and hard. "If I knew that I'd be doing it, wouldn't I? We're going to have to hang around until we get the results from running the plates. Nothing we can do until they come through."

Des wandered back to the vehicle and stuck his head inside the car. "I think we're good to move the corpse now. Mitch, I need you guys to give me a hand. Why don't you get in the passenger seat? You can assist us from that side while we ease the victim out."

"Want us to keep an eye on the plastic sheet?" Sam asked, eager to lend a hand, but she was conscious about keeping out of the way at the same time.

"That'd be great. It's likely to blow away in this wind."

The team gathered around, took their instructions from Des, and within a few minutes they had eased the victim from the car and placed the body on the sheeting that Sam and Bob had pinned down with their feet.

Des got down on his knees to examine the remains. It wasn't long before he declared, "The victim is a male. Judging by the wedding band on his left hand, he's married."

Bob's phone rang seconds later. He answered the call and said, "We've got a possible victim's name, Alvin Davidson."

"And an address?" Sam asked.

"Yes. Tidy End Farm out at Camerton."

"Brilliant news. One last thing, Bob, can you check with

the station, see if there has been a missing person report filed for the victim?"

"Will do." Bob made the call.

"We'll get him back to the lab, and I'll start the PM straight away," Des said.

"Why don't you leave it until later? It's not like he's going anywhere, is it? You need to get some rest, Des. And spend some time with that wonderful family of yours."

"Some hope of that happening anytime soon. No, I'll perform the PM and hopefully get my head down for a few hours. That'll probably be at the office, though."

"Your wife is going to think she has a stranger in the house when you finally get home. You need your time off, just like the rest of us, Des. What if you made a costly mistake during a post-mortem?"

"I'm not likely to, so stop worrying. You live your life and I'll live mine."

"Sorry, I didn't mean to lecture you, I'm just concerned you're going down a slippery slope, that's all. You need another assistant."

"They're hard to come by, and the last one wasn't much cop, was she?"

"She was. You being you, and in your infinite wisdom, just didn't give her a chance."

"You have your opinion on that, and I have mine. We've spoken about this before, Sam, she wasn't cut out for the job. I can't keep carrying people who drive me to distraction."

Sam knew when to back off and not to push things. "Okay, we'll agree to differ on that one. She's doing well by the way. I saw Kathryn a few days ago, and she loves her new job."

"I hear she's had several since giving in her notice with us."

"She has but she's far happier in herself."

"Job satisfaction has always been at the top of my agenda, Sam, it always will be. I also need people around me who I can rely on. She was far from reliable."

Sam shrugged. "I thought she was great to put up with your grouchiness the way she did. You should consider taking her back. At least you found some time to spend with your family while she was around."

Des narrowed his eyes at her and growled. "Time to get this one back to the lab," he said to his team, dismissing Sam.

She sniggered and walked back to her car. Sam and Bob removed their suits and shoe covers and placed them in the black sack close to the cordon.

"You're taking a risk, winding him up like that," Bob whispered in her ear.

"They say the truth hurts. I've planted the seed. He'll chew it over during the day. We'll see if he acts upon it."

"It could go one of two ways."

"Such is life, it's fraught with dilemmas. I've had a fair few to deal with myself over the years."

"Haven't we all?" Bob grumbled.

She dug him in the ribs. "Let's not dwell on things and get maudlin. Shall we take both cars?"

"Might as well. You'll be whacking the heater up full blast in yours, whereas I prefer to be able to breathe in mine."

"You know me so well. Do you know where we're going?"

"I've got a rough idea. Want me to take the lead?"

She grinned. "You read my mind. Don't rush, I need to gather my thoughts during the journey."

"I don't envy you," he said and dipped into his car.

They left the scene and drove to the farm. It took around fifteen minutes to get there. By that time, Sam had collected her thoughts but still wasn't feeling confident about breaking the devastating news. The reason behind her hesitation was obvious, to her anyway. Losing her mother recently and how that news had impacted her daily life. Yes, it was getting easier day by day, however, a certain song on the radio, or a memory filling her mind, sometimes had the ability of stopping her dead in her tracks. So much so that she had barely listened to the radio in her car since the funeral just in case one of the songs they had used started playing and she ended up a blubbering mess.

Just thinking about her dear mother some days was enough to make her eyes water.

She inhaled a steadying breath and left her vehicle. Bob stood on the pavement, staring at her.

"I've been watching you in my mirror. Are you up to this, Sam?"

She touched his cheek. "Thank you for caring. I'm okay. It's getting easier, but I'm still not a hundred percent yet. I promise it won't affect my performance."

"Performance? You get one shot at this, Sam. If you're not up to the task, I could step in."

She staggered backwards and dramatically slapped a hand to her chest. "Is the great Bob Jones telling me he's willing to deal with a family's grief head-on?"

"Don't take the piss."

"Sorry, I didn't mean to. Don't worry about me, I'll be fine. Shoulders back, and here we go."

"I don't want to leave it there, Sam. Are you sure you're okay? Because you don't look it, and I know how upsetting this process can be for you ordinarily, without the extra baggage you're carrying at present."

"Honestly, whilst your worrying is commendable, it's totally uncalled for. Now, can we get in there before my nerve goes or you end up giving me a complex?"

"I'm sorry, that wasn't my intention. If you're struggling at any time, just give me the nod and I'll take over, got that?"

"I've got it. Thanks, partner. Let's do this. There's a light just gone on in the lounge, which is a relief. I thought we'd have to wake them up."

The curtain was pulled back, and a young woman peered out at them and gasped. Sam smiled and strode up the garden path with Bob close behind her.

"Good luck," he whispered.

The door opened, and Sam whipped out her ID. "Hello, are you Mrs Davidson? I'm DI Sam Cobbs, and this is my partner, DS Bob Jones."

"I'm *Miss* Davidson, sorry, Jenny. Is this about my father?"

"Is your mother around?"

"No, she passed away years ago. Dad remarried Bethany, she's upstairs having a lie-down. We've both been pacing the floor all night, waiting for my father to come home. You're worrying me. Is he all right?"

"Can we come in and speak with you?"

"Yes, of course. I'd better give Bethany a shout." Jenny took a few steps back and went to the bottom of the stairs. "Bethany, are you awake?"

"Yes, what is it, Jenny? Is that your father home now?"

"No, it's two police officers to see us. Can you come down, please?"

A thump sounded overhead, followed by thudding on the landing until a woman in her fifties appeared at the top of the stairs. "Have you found him? We've been worried sick about him all night, haven't we, Jenny?"

"Yes. Are you coming down? I'll take them into the lounge. It must be important if they've come to see us at this hour."

Sam issued a half-smile. "Will you join us, Bethany?"

The woman ran a hand around her face and through her already messed-up hair. "I'll... be right down." Then she disappeared again.

"Come through. She'll be up there, making herself look

more presentable. I suppose I should ask you if you want a drink," Jenny said.

They followed the young woman into the lounge, and she gestured for Sam and Bob to take a seat on the sofa.

"Not for us, but thanks for asking," Sam replied.

A few minutes later, once the three of them were seated, Bethany entered the room. Her hair, dyed blonde, had been brushed, and she had changed out of her dressing gown and pyjamas into a skirt and jumper.

"Well, I asked if you'd found him, and you ignored me. Have you?" Her anger was directed at Sam.

"Take a seat," Sam insisted.

Bethany fell into the armchair behind her. "It isn't good, is it? For God's sake, just tell us."

"Yes. Unfortunately, what we believe to be your husband's car was found last night. There was a body inside the vehicle. We won't be able to give you a definitive answer if it is him yet, not until the pathologist has performed the post-mortem."

The two women stared at each other. Jenny was the first to break down. She hid her head in her hands and sobbed. It took Bethany several moments to do the same as if shock had caused the delay.

Sam watched on, and Bob crossed and uncrossed his ankles a few times while they waited for the sobbing to die down.

"Can I get either of you a drink, to possibly help soften the blow?" Sam asked.

Sitting up erectly, pushing her shoulders back, Bethany nodded. "I'd like a strong cup of tea. How about you, Jenny?"

"No, all I want is… my father back."

Bethany pushed herself to her feet and shook her head. "Well, that's not likely to happen, is it? We're going to have to get used to the idea that he's no longer with us, and quickly."

Bethany breezed out of the room, and Jenny continued to sob.

Sam took a gamble; she left the lounge and went in search of Bethany. She found her standing by the back door, smoking a cigarette.

"It's an addiction I've never really been able to kick. Filthy habit and costs a fortune, but I don't drink, so I fail to see any harm in it. I mean, I know it's harmful to smoke, what I meant was that I can't see any harm *in me* doing it. Although it used to tick my husband off, more and more each day. So much so that come the end, I had to resort to smoking in secret. I guess I no longer need to do that now, do I?"

Sam smiled and approached the woman. "You do what you feel you need to do to cope with the situation. We all deal with grief differently."

"Voice of experience talking, is it?"

"Yes, I lost my mother around three months ago. I'm not saying it has been easy since her death, but I've coped."

"How did she die?"

"She had a brain tumour. They tried their best to operate on it, but it proved to be impossible come the end."

"I'm sorry to hear that. I lost my mother when I was only five. My miserable excuse for a father brought me up, when he wasn't necking pint after pint down the pub. He left me alone in the house for hours at night until he finally staggered home, and then he beat the crap out of me if I dared to challenge him."

"That's terrible. Did you have any siblings?"

"Yes, Mum gave birth to two babies, one when I was three and the other when I was four. They both died after only living a couple of days. Mum couldn't deal with the loss, not after the second baby died. She killed herself, stabbed herself in the heart one day. My father kind of rejected me after that. I suppose he blamed me for their deaths."

"What? But you were a mere child, how could you have possibly had anything to do with them dying?"

"Exactly. He despised me for years until he finally stumbled into the road on his way home from the pub one night and a car, or was it a lorry? No, I think it was a car, ran him over. He was killed instantly. I had just turned eighteen and was all alone. No other family members stood beside me at his funeral. I've never felt that alone before or since."

The kettle finished boiling. She stubbed out her cigarette on the exterior wall, closed the back door and walked across the room. "Do you and your partner want a drink? Have you changed your mind?"

"Okay, two white coffees with one sugar, please. Let me do it for you."

"I'm fine. I'd rather keep my hands busy." Bethany removed four mugs from the tree and proceeded to place either a tea bag or a spoonful of coffee in each of them, followed by sugar. "Jenny doesn't usually take sugar, but I think the sweetness will help deaden the pain. Poor girl, what on earth is she going to do now, without her father? I'm not much of a stand-in, not with my past. I've done my best for her over the years, but I've always felt it wasn't good enough for either of them."

"I'm sure that's not the case. It's often difficult to adapt taking on someone else's child to raise. How old was Jenny when you married your husband?"

"A teenager, just. She was thirteen."

"And how old is she now?"

"Twenty-three or is she twenty-four? I can never remember, and time flies by, I'm sure you'll agree."

"Absolutely. You appear to get on well together."

"We do. Teenagers can be a handful to deal with. Alvin insisted I should handle any female issues with her myself, although she had other plans and refused to take my advice where boyfriends et cetera were concerned. It is what it is. I wasn't going to sit there and force her to be my friend or take any advice I had to offer her. I was as much out of my depth in that department as she was. No one was on hand to guide me through that period of my life. I had to grow up quickly."

"I'm sorry to hear that. Jenny seems well adjusted. Do you get on with her?"

"Yes, most of the time. We've had our moments over the years. You tell me a family who hasn't had issues, and I'll buy them a trip to the North Pole to visit Santa next year."

Sam smiled. "I suppose that's true. Can I help you with those?"

"If you don't mind."

Sam couldn't help but notice how Bethany was taking the news of her husband's death in her stride, compared to how Sam had reacted to her own mother's death. It was true, how every person accepted and dealt with their grief differently. She assisted Bethany, collected the two mugs containing coffee and returned to the lounge with her. Bob's gaze latched on to Sam's. She could tell he was way out of his depth, being left alone with Jenny. The relief was written on his face when she and Bethany returned to the lounge. Jenny dabbed at her eyes and then blew her nose on a fresh tissue, her grief clear for everyone to see. Sam passed Bob his drink, which he cradled in both of his hands.

"Where... was... he... found?" Jenny said between shuddering breaths.

"His car was discovered on the industrial estate out at Stainburn. Can you tell us at what time he left the house and where he was going?"

Bethany stared at the wall for a long moment and then told them, "I'm not sure. I think he left home at around four yesterday. He had a part to pick up for the ride-on lawn mower. He was also going to fill up the petrol canisters to enable him to do some work with the strimmer in one of the fields. We're reliant on the dry days at this time of the year to get the little jobs completed, such as keeping the gates clear here and there, so we're able to move the livestock around."

"I see. Did he contact you while he was out?"

"No. He had no reason to. I trusted my husband was going to be where he said he was. Are you telling me that I should ring him every hour, on the hour, when we're not together, like most women do? Give a man his freedom once in a while and he's less likely to stray, wouldn't you agree, Inspector?"

"I've never really thought about it that way before, Mrs Davidson. Do you know the name of the shop where he was due to pick up the part?"

"I don't. I wouldn't have thought there are too many of them around there, so it should be easy for you to trace, using your detective skills." Bethany sighed and took a sip from her mug.

Sam's gaze drifted between the two women. Jenny had calmed down considerably by now. Her sobbing had turned into the odd sniffle, but her tears still continued to flow and stain her cheeks.

"Was he going to stop off anywhere else while he was out? I'm asking because of the timeline involved. You said your husband left here at around four. It would have taken him approximately twenty to twenty-five minutes to get to Stainburn, depending on the traffic at that time of the day. A further thirty minutes maximum sourcing and collecting the part, and yet his car was found at around seven last night, in flames."

Jenny screamed, scaring the shit out of Sam. "No. Is that how he died?"

Sam nodded. "I'm sorry, yes. The car was engulfed in

flames by the time a passing motorist raised the alarm. It was too late to save Mr Davidson."

Bethany sat there, silently sipping her drink and shaking her head. The odd tear slipped onto her cheek. "No. Oh my, I can't believe what we're hearing. How awful for Alvin, your father, to go out that way. Do you think he would have realised what was going on? Would the explosion have been instant, or do you think he tried to deal with the fire and got caught out?"

"It's hard to tell how the incident happened at this stage. Scenes of Crime Officers are doing their utmost to find any clues there might be around his vehicle. What I can tell you is that his body was found inside the car."

"Noooo…" Jenny cried out. "Are you saying that he burned to death? When you said the car was engulfed in flames… well, I presumed, or I'd hoped, he managed to get out of the car before anything drastic could happen to him. Are you telling us that isn't the case?"

Sam shook her head. "Sorry, no. It would appear your father failed to leave the vehicle before the fire took hold."

"I can't believe what I'm hearing," Bethany whispered, her gaze drawn to her stepdaughter, who was obviously struggling to deal with the truth.

"Going back to the timeline, is there anywhere else he was planning to go yesterday?"

"Not that I can think of," Bethany said. "Maybe he stopped off at the pub for a sneaky pint. That wasn't unheard of, was it, Jenny?"

"No, I mean yes, he sometimes did that, if it was close to the end of the day. I thought he would have been back earlier. I went out at around six. I had an evening class at the college to attend."

"What are you studying, anything interesting?" Sam asked.

"I think it is. I'm learning how to paint from scratch. I'm enjoying the challenge of learning a new skill."

Bethany pointed at a picture on the wall to the left, over her shoulder. "That's one of Jenny's. Her father had been so proud of her when she presented it to him for his birthday a few months ago."

Jenny sobbed again. "It was the first time I'd been truly happy with my work. I told him when I started the course that when that day came, I would gift him the piece I was working on, for a keepsake."

Sam placed her mug on the coaster on the table and rose to her feet to get a closer look at the picture. It was a farm scene, a red tractor parked in front of a couple of barns and a man standing alongside it. "Is that your father?"

"Yes. His tractor was his pride and joy. I wanted to paint something he would be proud of, and he was. He told me it was the best present anyone had ever given him. He got choked up at the time, didn't he, Bethany?"

"He did. He was thrilled with the gift. As I recall, he wouldn't stop going on about it for months."

Sam returned to her seat on the sofa. "You definitely have a talent for painting, Jenny."

"Thank you. I'm not sure if I'll continue with the course now."

"May I ask why?" Sam asked, shocked by the young woman's admission.

"Because I was planning to create a collection of paintings, featuring the farm. I can't see the point of doing that now that my father has gone. This was his dream, not ours. Isn't that right, Bethany?"

"It was, love. I'm not sure what will happen to this place now he's gone. I don't suppose we'll be able to cope on our own, and Mick isn't getting any younger, is he?"

"No, that's right. I'm sure he will help out and do extra hours if we begged him to."

Sam inclined her head. "Mick? I take it he's one of the employees?"

"Yes, sorry, he's worked here for years, before I came on the scene. They had a good working relationship and were best of friends; it was more like a bromance," Bethany said, her face lighting up at the memories which had surfaced.

"Can we get his details from you? Does he work here full-time?"

"Yes, he's here more than he's at home with his wife, which doesn't go down too well with Tara. They have two children, aged seven and eight. She's always complaining that he barely sees them for more than a few minutes every day. Alvin was trying to come up with a solution for that because it was beginning to get Mick down... now this. Oh God, what if he throws in the towel and ups and leaves us? Where will we be then, Jenny?"

"Up the bloody creek. This place used to run like clockwork for two reasons, because of the way Dad and Mick worked it. All that has gone to pot now. What's that going to mean for us? I can't give up my job and help out around here."

"What do you do, Jenny?" Sam jumped in, trying to pick up snippets of the conversation before it spun off in a different direction as these types of things had a habit of doing.

"I work as a hairdresser and I'm good at it. I've won a couple of awards both locally and nationally."

Sam smiled. "That's impressive. Have you been doing it long?"

"About seven years. I left school at sixteen, got an apprenticeship at the best salon in town. I attended college at the same time. My boss is always telling me I have a natural ability to cut hair."

"She's a very clever girl when she puts her mind to it," Bethany agreed. "However, once there's a young man on the scene, all common sense goes out of the window, doesn't it, Jenny?"

The young woman dipped her head. "I know. It's what pissed Dad off the most."

"Do you have a boyfriend now?"

"No, the last one ran off with one of my so-called friends. Good luck to them, they're well suited. Back-stabbing gits, the pair of them. I can do without toxic people like that in my life."

"Always a good idea, clearing out the friendships that no longer give us satisfaction," Sam said. "Is there anyone who has caused any trouble for Alvin lately?"

"Trouble, in what respect?" Bethany asked. She took a sip from her drink and then placed her mug on the table beside her.

"Any problems here at the farm? What about other members of the family, any reason to be concerned there?"

"No, there's only us three. Alvin's parents died years ago; he inherited the farm. His brother used to help out around here, although that was debatable at times. He never gave the farm his undivided attention, not like Alvin did."

"Used to? Is he no longer around?"

"No. He died a few years back. It was awful, a tragic accident. I was out there, helping with the harvest one day," Bethany said in a shaky voice. "I'd got in the tractor and lost control of it. I hit reverse and ended up flattening Stuart. He came from nowhere. One minute he was on the other side of the yard, and the next, right behind me. The visibility on tractors isn't the best. Yes, you're high up and should be able to see all around you, but you still have blind spots. I was devastated, and Alvin struggled to get over the loss."

"I'm so sorry to hear that. Did he have any family of his own?"

"Yes, his wife, Fiona, used to live here at the farm. She was traumatised by the events and ended up going all the way home to Devon to be with her parents. She was pregnant at the time. She cut off all contact with us, couldn't bring herself to talk to us, which really hurt, didn't it, Jenny?"

"It did. I'm dying to know if she gave birth to a boy or girl. I guess we'll never know. It's been about three years since Stuart died. I don't suppose she'll bother getting in touch with us again now," Jenny said, her shoulders sinking in despair.

"It's a shame when family members walk away like that," Sam said. "Grief can be a bugger to deal with for some people. It must have been a hell of a shock for her. Did you all get along, up until Stuart's death?"

"Yes, we were all very close," Jenny was the first to respond.

"As Jenny said, we all got on really well, as a family who spent most of their time together, working on the farm."

"And they lived here as well? In the farmhouse?"

"No, the parents converted one of the barns for Stuart to live in with his family. We rent it out occasionally. Not too often, because it can take a lot of hard work to see to people's needs. Nothing ever seems to go right in that place, there's always a leak to deal with or something that needs maintaining and isn't up to some people's standards," Bethany replied. She rolled her eyes and blew out a breath. "Running a holiday business isn't all it's cracked up to be, and don't get me started on the damage some of these individuals cause. It's not for the faint-hearted, or for those who take pride in their accommodation. I've always said that people tend to leave their brains at home when they go on holiday."

"I've heard that said before," Sam said. "One of my friends rented out her gîte when she moved to France a few years back. She regretted that decision after only having three or four couples stay at the property. She was thankful when the season finished. She told me she was on the verge of having a nervous breakdown."

"I'm not in the least bit surprised. That's why we rarely rent it out now, and then only to people who have stayed here before, who we can trust will take care of the place. It's not much to ask, is it? What happened to your friend?"

"She decided to forget about the holidaymakers and now rents it out to a local full-time and has never had an issue since."

"Good for her. Maybe that's something we can look at doing, Jenny? We're going to need some form of rental or steady income coming in, now that your father is no longer with us."

"Do we have to think about that at this time, Bethany, can't it wait?"

"I'm sorry. Ever the practical one. Of course, you're right, and I'm totally in the wrong. Please forgive me, all of you. My mind is constantly whirring, always planning ahead, that's my trouble."

"There's no need to apologise," Sam said. "Having a practical plan in place might help you deal with your loss better."

"Possibly, but it was still the wrong time for me to discuss how we're going to survive after losing Alvin." Bethany bowed her head in shame.

"You mentioned that Alvin was going to pick up supplies, such as fuel for the lawn mower. Did he have a preference for which garage he used?"

"Not as far as I know. Jenny, can you think of one?"

"Knowing him, he'd drive around Workington, looking for the cheapest, just to save a penny or two, not taking into consideration how much the trip was likely to cost him."

Sam smiled. "Must be a male trait. My father does the same, especially nowadays, with the price of fuel going up weekly. Does he have a pub he prefers to use? You mentioned he might have stopped off for a sneaky pint on his way back."

"Yes, that's probably what happened, if he got all his chores done early. He sometimes stopped by the Farrier's Arms." Bethany clicked her finger and thumb together. "Yes, that's in Stainburn, or on the outskirts, isn't it, Jenny?"

"I think so. It's been a while since I ventured over that part of the town. I think the last time was when Dad gave me a lift to the station for a competition I'd entered."

"We'll drop by and have a word with the landlord or manager when they open later."

"What happens now?" Bethany asked. She plucked a tissue from the box beside her and wrapped it around a couple of her fingers.

"The post-mortem should take place today. The team will continue to search for any evidence at the scene, and our investigation will get underway as soon as we leave here. I must warn you that at the moment we've very little to go on. We're going to ask you to be patient with us. My team and I will do our best to get the case tied up as quickly as possible, but sometimes, in cases such as this, where the victim's body... has been badly damaged, shall we say? It can prove tricky to find out the cause of the death. But I want to assure you that we're going to give it our all."

"I see. And what about funeral arrangements? Will that be down to us in the circumstances?" Bethany asked. "I've never been in this situation before so I'm not sure what happens when a pathologist is involved."

"Okay, what usually happens is that once the PM has been

performed, the pathologist will release the body to the undertaker, however, in the case of a suspicious death, that release will more than likely be delayed for a few days, possibly longer. We will need to have a chat with the pathologist or see how things go with the PM before a decision can be made."

"So, do I start getting quotes from funeral directors or not?" Bethany asked.

Out of the corner of her eye, Sam saw Jenny discreetly shaking her head.

"What?" Bethany demanded. "If you have something to say, my girl, let's hear it."

"I don't. I know we have to be practical, but do we really need to discuss this when our feelings are so raw? I can't deal with it." Jenny then flew out of her chair and left the room, slamming the door behind her.

"Sorry, she's always been a sensitive child. I'm not sure I can handle her emotions and what I'm going through right now."

"Just deal with your own emotions, that should be your priority at this time."

"Thank you, I'm going to try." Bethany's hand touched her face, and she turned her head away from Sam. "I have no idea how we're going to cope. The farm isn't the easiest business to run. The new rules and regulations the government has forced upon us, since Brexit, are restrictive to say the least. But we coped, just, together, but now I'm all alone. I know the light at the end of the tunnel is going to be out of reach some days more than others."

"You'll get there. Jenny seems a likeable and conscientious young lady, I'm sure she'll lend a hand when she can, either after work or at the weekends perhaps."

"Saying it and doing it are two completely different things." Bethany's head dropped again. "How am I ever going to cope? It's hard enough to deal with a person's death without the added worry of dealing with a business on top."

"I'm so sorry of what lies ahead of you, especially with the investigation adding to your woes. If there's ever anything I can do for you, just give me a shout."

"You can find out how my husband died, and if his death is suspicious, who killed him, if that's where your investigation is leading."

"As I said earlier, we're going to need time, but I promise you that we won't leave any stone unturned. We never have and never will, not on my watch."

"Thank you, that's good to know. I should go and see where Jenny has got to now."

"You do that. We're going to make a move, if that's all right with you?"

"Yes, of course. There's no point in you hanging around here with us, not when there's a murderer out there who needs to be caught. Will you leave me your card?"

Sam had already removed one from her jacket pocket in anticipation. "Here you go. Ring me day or night with any queries you might have or if you think of anything that we should take a further look at."

"I will. I'm glad we have you available to support us. I think we have a tough road ahead of us, Inspector, and I'm sure there are going to be days when we'll be walking around in a daze, unsure what to do for the best."

"Don't hesitate to get in touch if that should happen."

They all stood and walked out of the lounge.

Bethany saw them to the front door and shook their hands. "I feel confident that we have the right person in charge of the investigation, and I want to thank you for that, Inspector."

"Thank you, that means a lot to us. I'll be in touch soon. Take care of each other. Try and get some rest when you can.

I'm aware how difficult that is going to possibly be for you, what with running the farm as well as going through the grieving process."

Bethany nodded. "I haven't got a clue what to expect over the coming days, but at least I'm not alone and will have Jenny by my side throughout this dreadful ordeal."

Sam and Bob left the house. They reached the cars, and Sam glanced at her watch.

"We were there longer than expected, it's coming up to eight-thirty now. Have you eaten?"

"No. I was worried my stomach was going to embarrass me and start growling back there. What are you thinking?"

"That we stop off at a greasy spoon café on the way back. There are a couple on the outskirts of town, not that I've ever had the pleasure of using either of them before. Do you know what they're like?"

"Yeah, I've been to Joe's Gaff, but it was a few years ago. I couldn't vouch for the quality of his sausage these days."

Sam laughed and felt guilty, given her surroundings. "That tickled me far more than it should have."

"A sausage tickling a woman, who would have thought it," Bob retorted with a straight face.

Sam sniggered. "You lead the way."

They jumped into their respective vehicles. Sam glanced at the farmhouse as she circled the driveway and noticed Bethany at the window upstairs, watching them leave. Sam waved, but the woman turned her back.

Did she see me or not? Who knows what goes on in some people's heads once grief sets in?

CHAPTER 2

*B*ob volunteered to pay for breakfast. He had the works, a large full-English while Sam plumped for a bacon roll. Rather than twiddle her thumbs in Bob's absence, she dialled Rhys' mobile, but it rang out. She gave up trying to contact him when Bob returned to the table and sat opposite her.

"Sorry, did I interrupt your call?"

"No, there was no answer. Rhys is probably out walking the dogs and left his phone at home."

"Part-timer. What time does he generally head off to work?"

"About eight-forty-five."

"Are you worried about him?"

"No, not really. Not when there's a logical explanation to be had. How long is our breakfast going to be?"

"Your bacon roll should be with you shortly. My masterpiece will take a while to throw together." His stomach rumbled loudly.

"Not a moment too soon by the sounds of it," Sam said. Her mobile rang. "Hey, were you out with the dogs?"

"I took them out early this morning, I had trouble getting back to sleep after you left. Umm… I took Sonny next door to Doreen."

"Is everything all right?"

"Yes, she told me not to tell you."

"Tell me what? Come on, Rhys, you can't leave me dangling like that."

"She had a slight fall this morning. I told her I would take care of Sonny, but she insisted she wanted to look after him."

"Oh bugger, how bad is it?"

"She was hobbling on a swollen ankle."

"Damn, I could have asked Vernon to watch Sonny today, had I known."

"That would have upset her, love. She assured me she was fine and was determined to stick to her usual routine."

"Okay, I'll pick her up a bunch of flowers and some chocolates on the way home. She's getting some fuss whether she likes it or not."

"There's no point in me advising you against it, is there?"

"Nope, my mind is made up."

"How are you? And how is the investigation going?"

"We haven't really got started yet. All we've done so far is visit the scene and then share the news with the family. Bob and I are sitting in a café, about to have breakfast before we head to the station."

"Ah, I see. Okay, I've nearly reached work now, I'll see you later. Take care, love you."

"Love you, too. Have a good day, Rhys."

Sam placed her phone on the table and muttered, "Damn."

"Everything all right?" Bob asked.

"Not really. Doreen, my neighbour, has had a fall and twisted her ankle."

"The lady who cares for Sonny while you're at work?"

"That's the one. I always feel guilty putting on her when she's not well. I refuse to do it when she's injured herself. I have to make other arrangements later. Will you remind me?"

"Of course."

The waitress delivered Sam's bacon roll, and Bob's breakfast arrived a couple of minutes after that.

Sam tore into the roll and let out a moan of pleasure.

"Do you mind? We're getting funny looks. Are you practicing your Meg Ryan impersonation?"

"It's delicious, what more can I say? It's been a while since I've had a bacon roll of this quality."

"Oh God, does that mean we're going to be forced to visit this place regularly from now on?"

"Possibly. Yours looks super, not that I can eat that much in the morning. I hope it doesn't slow you down, we've got lots to do when we get back."

"Don't worry, it won't. I'll probably be ready for another one in an hour or so."

"Bloody hell. A breakfast as big as that would see me through the rest of the day. Anyway, let's get back to work. What do you make of the grieving widow?"

"Hard to tell. Her emotions appeared to be all over the place. One minute she was sobbing her heart out, and the next she had her practical head on. Can't tell from that what's going on. Now the daughter, Jenny, well, that's a different story entirely. My heart went out to the girl. Saying that, he was her father, so she's bound to be feeling it more, isn't she?"

"Yeah, I guess so. Had we delivered the news to them separately, I doubt if I would be thinking anything of it. I'm prepared to give Bethany some slack for now. For all we know, she might be the type to put on a front, and once the curtains are closed, she'll probably collapse in a heap."

"I bet you've hit the nail on the head there. Not sure how they're going to cope running that place."

"Correction, she, the stepmother, because Jenny has a full-time job elsewhere."

"It's a shame they don't have any other staff to help them, other than this Mick who we still need to have a chat with."

"It's going to put them under more pressure. Farming is an all hours and all types of weather job, which I should imagine is far from easy." Sam took a sip of her coffee and pushed her empty plate to the side. "That was delicious. We'll definitely call again if ever we're in the area."

Bob continued to wolf down his breakfast and nodded.

"So, the next job on the agenda is to visit the pub. We'll drop by and see if anyone is there after we've had breakfast. We might be in luck, sometimes the owner or manager lives on the premises."

"I don't know the pub in question, so I can't say either way."

When they arrived at the pub around fifteen minutes later, the car park was empty and the curtains were drawn closed. Sam knocked on the door at the side of the property, just in case but, as suspected, no one answered. She jumped in the car and drove back to the station with Bob close behind her.

There, she ran through the case with the rest of the team, put them to work, trying to find out what they could about the farmer, and then she went into her office to deal with the post that had appeared overnight.

Job completed, at ten-thirty, Sam collected Bob and headed back to the pub.

"Looks like we're in luck this time."

There were now two vehicles parked in the far corner of the car park.

"Fingers crossed."

They left the car. The main door was ajar. Bob knocked on the inner door and opened it when a man's voice invited them to enter.

Sam smiled at the man stocking up the bar. "Hi, I'm DI Sam Cobbs, and this is my partner, DS Bob Jones. Are you the manager?"

"Yes, well, the owner. I'm Terry, and this is Anne, my partner. What brings the police to our door?"

"We're conducting enquiries into a serious crime that we believe has been committed."

He paused what he was doing and approached the bar. "What? Here? Is that what you're suggesting?"

"No, not at all. We believe the victim may have stopped off here for a drink last night."

"Oh, victim? As in someone has died? Or as in they were badly injured?"

"Sadly, the victim lost their life last night."

"That's a bummer. Who? Are they a regular, or did they drop in on the off-chance?"

"The victim's name is Alvin Davidson, do you know him?"

"Shit, yes, we know him, don't we, Anne?"

"Yes," Anne replied. She stopped filling the fridge and came to join them. "He doesn't come in that often, not as much as he used to. Pleasant chap, never had an issue with him at all, have we, love?"

"No bother at all. What happened to him? Get mugged on the way home or something along those lines, did he?"

"If only. No, his car burst into flames. Unfortunately, he never made it out."

"Holy shit! What caused the fire, do you know?"

"We've yet to find the source. SOCO are out there now, going over the scene."

"Poor bloke. How can we help?"

"Perhaps you can tell us if Mr Davidson visited the pub last night?"

"Yes, he only popped in for a swift one. That's all it ever is these days, now that he's remarried. Up until he met, God, what's her name now?"

"Bethany, I believe," Anne filled in for him.

"That's right. We've never met her. He's not really one for going out socialising apparently. I don't suppose they get much time off. Farming is hard work at the best of times, let alone in the midst of winter. I can't believe I'm not going to see his smiling face again."

"How often did he drop in?"

"Once in a blue moon lately. He never altered, though, still the same happy-go-lucky type of chap."

"Do you recall what time he was here last night?"

"He came in at about five-thirty, at a guesstimate. Stayed for about an hour, maybe slightly longer, and then left."

"Yes, he was talking to old Fred and a few of the others. He didn't seem to be in that much of a hurry to leave. If anything, I'd say he was a tad reluctant to go."

Sam inclined her head. "What gave you that impression, Anne?"

The woman shrugged. "I can't put my finger on it. I reckon he was having a laugh with the others and possibly missed the old days, you know, when he was able to come here and while away the hours, within reason. I'm not saying he was a heavy drinker and drove home drunk every night. A pint would last him a while, though."

"I understand. Just to confirm, neither of you have met his wife, is that correct?

"No, she's never set foot in the place. His daughter used to come in with him now and again. Christ, I bet she'll be cut up about his death. They were really close," Terry said.

"I see Jenny regularly, she's even cut my hair a few times at the salon," Anne said. "Yes, she's a lovely girl, very inoffensive. Devoted to her father. I believe she helps out at the farm a lot during the busy spells. When the evenings are lighter and at the weekend. I think she'd like to work there full-time, from what I could tell, but it wouldn't be financially viable for her to do it, hence her taking on the job at the salon. She's a clever girl, won certificates for her work. She'd be foolish to ignore a talent like that. Her father was extremely proud of her achievements."

"And her stepmother?"

Anne shrugged. "Hard to tell as we don't know her. He's never said anything bad about her, if that's what you're asking. Anything we've said here today is what we've picked up as a couple."

"That's fine. We're scrabbling around at the moment, searching for clues. Any insight you can give us into their relationship will remain confidential, I promise."

"We can't tell you much, not having met the woman," Anne said. "I didn't get the impression that their marriage was a bad one. Not like some who come in here. Some of the men spend all evening slagging off their wives or partners. You get a feel for what kind of a relationship some have by reading between the lines. I didn't pick up anything bad, not with Alvin and his wife."

"What about you, Terry?"

"Same goes for me as well."

"Is Fred a regular?" Sam asked.

"Yep, he'll be in here as soon as we open at eleven, never misses a day. He suffers from loneliness. His wife passed away a few years ago. It's not that he drinks a lot, he makes them last, it's the companionship he craves more than anything. She was everything to him. He and Alvin always got on well together. Used to wind each other up all the time, nothing malicious, just friendly banter. He's going to be devastated to hear the news about Alvin."

"Maybe we'll get a chance to see him if we stick around. I've noticed you have cameras dotted around the bar. I don't suppose you'd let us have a look at last night's recordings, would you?"

Terry and Anne glanced at each other.

"You do that," Anne said. "I'll leave the filling up for now and get changed and sort the till out. We can top up the drinks later, during a slow spell."

"If it's inconvenient, it can wait," Sam assured them.

"It's not. Go on, Terry, the quicker you get cracking…"

He tutted. "Bossy Boots has spoken. Why don't you come round, and I'll go through the discs with you?"

Sam smiled and followed Bob around the other side of the bar. Terry showed them through to an office at the rear of the property that was far from tidy.

"You'll have to excuse the mess, it's organised chaos, I promise."

Sam laughed. "It looks it."

"I'd offer you a seat, but it's buried under last year's accounts."

"Don't worry, we're fine."

Terry set the machine running and scrolled through the disc until Alvin appeared on the screen. "There he is. He came in, ordered a pint of bitter from Anne and wandered down to the other end of the bar and sat with young Fred. You'll see later that Andy and John joined them about ten minutes before Alvin announced he was leaving."

"I see. He seems pretty chilled, doesn't he, Bob?"

"Seems that way to me. Do you have any cameras outside the pub, overlooking the car park?"

"I have. Honestly, there's nothing to see here. I can whizz through the disc to show you the rest of it, if you like? I don't put up with crap in my pub so never get any hassle between the punters. They know they'd get barred if they caused any problems. I'm not here to referee their behaviour, I'm here to ensure they get served and have a good time."

"Well said. If we can view the footage from outside then, that'd be brilliant," Sam said.

He tapped a few buttons, and the image changed to show the car park. "Let's see if I can pick out his car on any of the cameras." The image changed on the screen until Terry pointed out a vehicle parked along the far wall. "There it is, at least I think it is. I can't get a close-up of his number plate but I'm sure that's his."

"Can we watch it for a few seconds, see if anyone tampers with it?"

"I doubt if they will, but sure." He busied himself tidying up some of the paperwork sitting on the desk.

Sam suspected the guilt was getting the better of him while he allowed Sam and Bob to view the footage as it happened.

"Hang on, what's this?" Bob said.

"What? I can't see anything. Where am I supposed to be looking, partner?"

Bob tapped the screen with his finger. "There's a dark figure on the other side of his car. They're being cautious, searching all around them. They seem shifty to me."

Terry joined in the conversation again. "You're right. Let me see if I can enhance the image for you." He pushed a few more buttons, and the camera shifted its angle a touch, but nothing too significant.

"There they are again. They're down by the tyres. Wait, now they're leaving. Can you switch views on the camera, Terry," Sam asked, her heart racing.

He tried his best. Unfortunately, the cameras lost sight of the person.

"Jesus, they've gone. No cars have left the area, so they probably parked on the main road. I bet there are no cameras on this stretch either," Bob said.

"You're right, there aren't," Terry agreed.

Sam bashed her clenched fist against her thigh. "Great, so we had the perpetrator right there, and now they've just vanished in the blink of an eye. Is it possible for you to give us a copy of the disc, Terry?"

"Of course. I'll get that sorted for you now. It's a bit cramped in here. Why don't you head back to the bar, and I'll be with you in a jiffy?"

"Sounds good to me. Thanks." Sam backed out of the room.

She and Bob returned to the bar.

"We need to check what state the tyres were in," Bob said. "I didn't think about that when we were at the scene this morning."

Sam nodded. "You're right, I'll contact Des now." She moved across the vast room and stood by the window to make the call. "Des, it's Sam Cobbs. Sorry to interrupt you, I have a question to ask that needs your immediate attention."

"Go on, surprise me."

"Can you tell if the tyres on Alvin's car have been tampered with?"

"We were just packing up, getting ready to leave. Let me take a wander over there. May I ask why?"

"Just something that has come up during our enquiries. Well?"

"Patience is a virtue, Inspector. I'm here now. The tyres have blown, due to the heat. Is that what you're referring to?"

"We're at the pub where Alvin was last night, and we've just viewed footage on the cameras of someone we suspect of tampering with the tyres."

"Okay, what I'm looking at is four tyres, all without their

caps on. It hadn't come to my attention before you mentioned it. I'll get the team to see if they can locate the caps. If not then, from what you've told me, it is likely they've been removed."

"Would that slow the car down whilst driving?"

"I don't think so, I've had a tyre work okay with a missing cap before. Saying that, the perpetrator might have let some air out as they removed the caps; that would have slowed the car down, caused a warning light to appear. Maybe the victim got worried, pulled over to check everything was all right, and the perpetrator took the opportunity to pounce upon him."

"What we're saying is the attack was premeditated, right?"

"If you insist, yes."

"Okay, it's something to go on. Keep looking for the caps."

"Amongst other evidence, we will. Is that it?"

"Yes, thanks for taking my call. We dropped over to the family earlier, shared the news. I'll send you an email with their details when I get back to the station."

"I'll look forward to receiving it, now I must get on. The weather is against us, again."

"Sorry for holding you up. Speak soon."

"I have no doubts about that, Inspector. Keep me informed if you discover anything else."

"I will." Sam ended the call and walked back to join the others. "He's checked the tyres, and the caps are all missing. He's going to ask the tech team to search the area for them in case they came off at the scene, after the car exploded."

"I think we both know the answer to that one," Bob replied.

Sam glanced at her watch; it was almost five to eleven. "Will we be in the way if we wait around for Fred to arrive?" she asked Terry.

"Go for it. Can I get you a drink?"

"An orange juice for me, if you don't mind?"

"And you, Bob?"

"I'll have the same." Bob dipped his hand in his pocket.

Terry refused to take the money offered. "I think I can stretch to a couple of juices."

Sam and Bob moved to the seats closest to the fire that was roaring in the hearth.

"Have you been here long, Terry?" Sam shouted across the room.

"About seven years. I started running the place and then got a loan from the bank to buy it a few years later, after the landlord retired."

"Are you busy?"

"We have our moments." He placed two glasses on a couple of coasters. "If you'll excuse me. Time's marching on, and we have a few things to tick off the list before we let the masses in. And yes, I'm joking. It'll only be Fred sitting at the bar for the first hour or so. Not worth opening some days, but I'd hate to let him down. He relies on us so much these days, poor bugger."

"Loneliness can eat away at your soul. You're doing a grand job watching out for him. I bet he regards this place as a lifeline." *Which reminds me, I need to check on Dad soon. I haven't heard from him for a few days.*

Terry cleaned a glass or two with a cloth and said, "He hasn't admitted it, but I believe you're right. It's about caring for those in the community, isn't it?"

"You're not wrong. Do you have a resident chef here?"

"Yes, we had to up his wages to keep him after the pandemic. He's been a godsend, and trade is picking up weekly, so worth the extra wages. Don't tell me you haven't sampled our menu yet? Take a gander, there's one on the next table."

Sam reached behind her and studied the menu, going

directly to the prices. "We'll have to pop in and see you over the weekend. Do you allow dogs?"

"Always, there's even a dog menu on offer, it's at the bottom there."

"Gosh, don't let my two hear you say that. I mean it, you'll have two new customers at the weekend. Is it best to book a table?"

"It's up to you, weekends are our busiest, so it might be wiser."

"Okay, a table for two at seven-thirty on Saturday, if you will?"

Terry flipped open a bookings' diary next to him. "How about seven-forty-five instead?"

"That'll do me. Thanks."

The door opened, and a wizened old man with a walking stick entered and glanced around. "Hey, this won't do, me not being the first to arrive."

They all laughed.

"Usual, is it, Fred?" Terry asked.

"Please, Terry. Would you like another drink?" Fred asked Sam and Bob.

"No, but that's very kind of you to offer," Sam replied.

"I'll get you your half of bitter, Fred, then I'll introduce you to the officers who'd like a chat with you."

"Officers? Of the law, is that what you said? You know my hearing isn't the best right now."

Sam approached the bar and stood next to the old man. "I'm Detective Inspector Sam Cobbs. It's nothing for you to be worried about, I promise."

"Good, because I'm not one for getting into trouble. Terry will vouch for me, won't you, son?"

"I will, Fred. Why don't you join the officers, and I'll bring your drink over to you?"

"I might agree if the beautiful Anne had said it. Any chance?" Fred winked, and they all laughed.

"Get away with you, I've told you before, she's spoken for."

"You have. Hey, you can't blame an eager octogenarian for trying, can you, lad?"

"Ever the optimist, Fred."

Sam accompanied the man to the table and sat in the seat next to him. He had a friendly face, a bit like her grandfather's.

"Now then, what's all this about?"

Terry deposited Fred's drink, much to the man's bemusement.

"My oh my, Anne, your hands have got terribly hairy overnight."

Terry tutted and made his way back to the bar.

"I love winding people up, in case you hadn't noticed."

"I figured that out by myself. How are you, Fred?"

His brow furrowed. "I'm fine. Excuse me, do I know you? You don't look familiar, but then, my ears aren't the only part of my anatomy suffering these days."

"No, you don't know me. Are you well?" she asked a second time, fearing his health wouldn't be up to what she was about to tell him.

"I'm as good as I'm going to be at my age. What's up, Inspector?" He rearranged his spectacles to sit more comfortably on the bridge of his nose.

Sam inhaled deeply and said, "How well do you know Alvin Davidson?"

"Good old Alvin and me, well, I reckon we go back a good twenty years or more. Why do you ask? Not been up to no good, has he?"

The way the man's face lit up rocked Sam to her core. She

was dreading revealing the truth. "Umm… I'm afraid I have some bad news for you, Fred."

He frowned. "What's that? Has he had an accident in that tractor of his?"

"No, it's nothing like that. His car was involved in an incident last night, and he…"

"No, don't tell me he's in hospital?"

"Sadly not, he didn't make it."

"Didn't make it? Are you telling me he's dead?"

"Unfortunately, he passed away during the incident."

"What are you talking about? You keep calling it an incident as opposed to an accident, may I ask why? You can come right out and say it, my ticker is in good nick. How did my good friend die?"

"We can't give a definitive answer to that question as yet. SOCO are still examining the vehicle and the surrounding area for evidence."

"I'm confused. I don't know what you're getting at. Was he killed?"

"Possibly. I'm sorry, I can't say more than that just now. What I'd like to ask you is if Alvin mentioned any problems he was having when he spoke to you last night."

Fred closed his eyes and shook his head. "No, I can't believe he's gone. Taken from us, for what? Who would do such a thing? Alvin has always been a really nice chap. Have you heard this, Terry?"

"I have, mate. Not the best news I've had this year. We'll have a drink on him before you go, all right?"

"I'll take you up on that. The inspector here is asking what Alvin was like last night. He was the same as normal, wasn't he?"

"Yep, that's what I told the inspector." Terry glanced at Sam. "Can I tell him what we saw on the camera?"

"What was that?" Fred asked. His head swivelled between Sam and Terry.

"When Terry kindly showed us the footage from the cameras overlooking the car park, we saw someone, dressed in black, tampering with his tyres."

"What?" Fred removed his glasses and rubbed his eyes, then slotted his spectacles into place once more. "That means it was a deliberate act then, doesn't it?"

"So it would appear. We can't make out who the perpetrator is from the footage, that's why we're asking those who chatted with him last night if they know anything. Whether Alvin shared any concerns with them."

"No. And I can tell you this for certainty, he wasn't acting any different than he did normally. This is shocking. I've lived eighty years in this world and have never had anyone I knew die in suspicious circumstances. I'm telling you now, I'm going to have trouble processing this news. It's deplorable that someone should target a decent man like Alvin. Do you have any idea who it could be?"

"I'm worried about you. Do you have anyone we can ring to come and stay with you?"

"Good grief, why would I want someone taking over my life? You don't think the person responsible is going to come after me next, do you?"

"No, that's not what I meant at all. I'm concerned, humour me. Let me call someone, just to stay with you overnight."

"No. That means no, not I'll think about it. I do fine on my own, with the help of Terry and Anne. They look after me well enough. I know it's not most people's idea of comfort, spending all their time at the local boozer, but it suits me."

"We'll take care of him, Inspector. If needs be, we have a spare room upstairs, but only if Fred wants to stay."

Fred's eyes teared up. "See what a super landlord he is? Nothing is too much trouble for our Terry. He'll regret offering me a bed for the night, though, because if I drink all day in his establishment, it has consequences during the night."

They all laughed.

"You're more than welcome, Fred, you know that," Anne confirmed.

"Thanks, everyone. It's not me you should be concerned about. You two should be out there hunting this person down, quick smart, not spending your time in here with us."

"We're just doing the groundwork first before we put our plans into action, Fred. Can you cast your mind back to the conversation you had with Alvin last night? Did he hint at anything not being right with him?"

"No, not that I could tell. He was his usual jovial self. No different to any other time when I've had a drink with him. I reckon, you're wasting your time, sitting around here, questioning us."

Sam sighed. "Okay, I agree. Thanks to all of you for putting up with us today. I'll see you on Saturday, Terry, with my other half in tow."

"We look forward to seeing you, Inspector. If we can be of further help with the investigation, you know where we are."

"You're too kind." Sam patted Fred on the forearm. "You take care of yourself, young man."

"I will. Can you let us know when you've captured this person?"

Sam nodded.

"Only I'd like to be standing outside the courthouse when they appear, throwing some bad tomatoes and eggs at them."

They all laughed again.

"I can just imagine you doing that." Sam smiled, gave his arm an extra squeeze, and then left the pub with Bob.

"Nice place and nice people," her partner noted once they were back in the car.

"All very nice, and even Alvin sounded a good sort of man, not the type to invite trouble to his door. If that's the case, why is he currently lying in the morgue, a charred mess?"

"Pass. It's beyond me. I'll tell you something else, too."

"What's that?"

"I'm betting we never find out who bumped him off either."

"Hey, it's not like you to give up before we've had a chance to get the investigation underway. I'm intrigued to know why you think that."

"Let's face it, the perpetrator did all they could to keep hidden from the cameras for a reason."

"And the reason for that was so no one would detect who they were and what they were up to. In other words, the attack or murder had probably been planned for either weeks or months, meaning the killer had been sitting and waiting for the opportunity to come their way."

"Exactly my thoughts. So where do we go from here?"

"The only option left open to us after speaking with his family and the people at the pub is to take it further, with a conference. Maybe we'll strike lucky and stir up a memory of Alvin having an argument with someone in public over the past couple of months."

"Sounds about right, if we want to get the investigation off the ground. Should we drop by the lawn mower specialists first?"

"Yes, we'll see what they have to say, if anything, and then shoot back to the farm to see if we can have a quick chat with Mick, the farmhand."

Someone has to know something, they just have to.

CHAPTER 3

Sam and Bob left the lawn mower business feeling frustrated and drove out to the farm once more.

"Well, that was a waste of time," Sam said.

"Yep, time and effort as well. I can't bear it when investigations grind to a bloody halt before they've got the chance to get underway. Is it worth us heading back out to the farm so soon?"

"I think it's imperative we have a chat with the person who probably spent most of their working day with Alvin, don't you?"

"If you put it that way. I still reckon we should put a conference out soon, though."

Sam drew into a lay-by she'd spotted up ahead and made the call. "Hi, Jackie, it's DI Sam Cobbs. Any chance you can set up a conference ASAP?"

"Hello, Sam. Umm... I've only this second agreed to air one today for another inspector. Will tomorrow do?"

"It'll have to. Okay, can you book the slot, and I'll have a chat with you later when I return to the station?"

"Consider it done. Shall we say midday tomorrow?"

"Sounds great to me. I'll work around it, if anything should crop up in the meantime."

"Great. I'll see you then, if not before."

Sam smiled at her partner and then indicated to pull out into the traffic once more. "Job done. He who hesitates and all that."

"Yeah, you've never been one for that, have you?"

"Nope, never have been and never will be. I've always been a strike-while-the-iron-is-hot kind of girl."

"No shit, Sherlock. Let's hope Mick can shed some light on what's going on. If not, I'm going to lose the will to live soon."

"PMA, partner. The key is not to let the negativity sink in."

"If you say so, hard not to sometimes."

"I know. But you know what they say, police work is about eighty percent of the time waiting for something to drop into your lap."

"Sounds like you've just made that saying up for me. Have you?"

"No comment." She smiled and took a right at the end of the road. They were two minutes away from the farm now.

"You're incorrigible."

"I've been called worse," she retorted, adding a laugh.

"You're presuming this Mick is at work. Why wasn't he there earlier? Don't farmers usually get up at the crack of dawn to tend to their animals?"

"They do, but he's a farmhand, not the owner of the farm. Maybe Alvin had him coming in later to give him a break and time for a rest before starting again later on in the day. It's a guess on my part, I don't profess to know how a farmer's schedule is arranged."

"Get you. I haven't got a clue either."

. . .

WHEN THEY ARRIVED, a man who Sam presumed to be Mick was walking across the farmyard, making his way towards one of the huge barns. He turned their way but didn't stop.

Sam got out of the car and shouted, "Mick? We'd like a chat with you, if you have the time?"

"Me? What for? I'm going to feed the pigs and then I need to go and see to the sheep. You're welcome to tag along, if you like?"

Sam glanced down at the new boots she was wearing. "We'll join you in a moment."

"You can't be serious," Bob shouted from the passenger seat.

"Get out. We'll put some booties over our shoes and boots, we'll be fine."

"You can buy me some new shoes if I need them."

"All right, there's no need to go on about it. We have a murder inquiry to solve, Bob, it shouldn't matter if we ruin a few pairs of shoes in the process."

"If you say so."

"I do." She opened the boot, extracted two pairs of booties and handed one set to her partner as he joined her.

"Should we put them on now or when the shit really hits us?"

"It's up to you. Maybe wait a little while. There's bound to be some grass around here for us to use to clean off most of the muck."

"You're all heart, boss."

"I know. Not every inspector would be as kind to you as I am."

"Whatever."

They headed towards the barn. The courtyard was passable, not too mucky, and inside, the barn had a layer of straw, soaking up most of the excrement from the animals. Sam decided to leave her covers off, but Bob, being a wuss, chose to protect his shoes.

"Abigail would kill me if I went home smelling of pig shit."

"Instead of talking it most of the time," Sam muttered a quick retort.

"I heard that."

She grinned. "I have news for you, you were meant to."

"What can I do for you?" Mick said.

Sam leaned on the metal railing surrounding the pigs who snorted joyfully as they munched on the pellets and veg Mick was feeding them.

Sam introduced Bob and herself. "I take it you've heard from Bethany about what's happened to Alvin?"

"I have. I was shocked and appalled to hear the news when I got here this morning."

"How are Bethany and Jenny holding up?"

"As well as can be expected. Jenny has taken it badly, but then I suppose she would. He was her father, and she'd known him longer."

"That's understandable. I need to ask you a few questions if you have the time?"

"I don't, not really. The animals still need feeding and cleaning out, that won't change just because someone has died."

"I get that. We're prepared to get messy for the cause if you're willing to put up with us following you around."

"It's up to you. What do you need to know?"

"If Alvin ever confided in you."

"All the time. In what respect?"

"I don't know, did he discuss any problems he was having?"

"Yes, he was having a lot, most of them to do with financing this place. It's an impossible task being a farmer these days with the new restrictions in place. We should be tending to the animals, not indoors, going over reams and reams of paperwork. It's about time this government woke up and realised what deep shit this country would be in if all the farms sold up. If you don't believe me, watch that *Clarkson's Farm*. I don't generally like the man and I know he screwed up a lot but give the man his due. He put the hours in only to make about twenty-five quid profit at the end of the year. That's shocking, and it's not far from the truth with a lot of farmers I know around here. The costs have escalated considerably over the last couple of years. Customers blame the farmers when we have to put our prices up, instead of blaming the government, you know, for the many screw-ups they keep making. Sorry, rant over."

Sam smiled. "You're entitled to rant. I don't think anyone could predict what a cock-up Brexit would be to our economy."

"We knew. We tried to fight against it, but no one in the government was prepared to listen, and look at them, they've got a revolving door in Downing Street. Not a single one of them worthy of the damn responsibility bestowed upon them. I apologise again. As you can tell, it's one topic that continues to rankle me once it's brought up."

"Don't worry. I'm not an expert on the subject, but my heart goes out to all those concerned. Maybe the pandemic has a lot to answer for as well."

"Yes, I'll give you that one. At the end of the day, it's a shitshow, but it's people like us, supplying produce to the country, who have to ultimately pay the price."

"It can't be easy for all concerned. Did Alvin mention if he was in any kind of debt?" Sam instantly wondered if a loan shark might be involved.

"I don't know the ins and outs, I just know that he was putting in even longer hours than before, trying to keep up with all the paperwork concerned with running a farm these days."

"And what about Bethany, did she help out?"

"Of course I did," a female voice shouted behind Sam. "What do you take me for? How dare you come here and accuse me of not pulling my weight. You don't know me from Adam, and yet here you are, slagging me off to the farmhand."

Sam groaned and turned to face her. "I'm sorry, you must have come in on the end of what I was saying. I didn't slag you off as you put it. All I'm trying to get to is the truth."

"Then you're asking the wrong person. It's me you should be talking to, not Mick. Why go behind my back and ask Mick as if I don't exist? Don't bother asking, I'm off back to the house to put in a complaint to your superiors."

Sam shrugged and watched the irate woman leave the barn. "As is her prerogative." She turned to face Mick.

He seemed gobsmacked by what he'd just witnessed.

"She didn't mean anything by it. She's lashing out, trying to find someone to blame for her loss," he said after a few moments' consideration.

"Don't worry. We meet all sorts and have to deal with all kinds of emotions in our job. Where were we? Ah yes, I was asking if Bethany did her fair share around the farm."

He raised an eyebrow and peered over Sam's shoulder to check the coast was clear. "She does her best, but I've never got the impression that her heart was ever in farming."

"How long has she been here?"

"Ten years they were married. I think he started seeing her a couple of months before. I know they didn't have a long courtship, not in the grand scheme of things."

"How did Alvin devote the time to dating? Or is that a dumb question when matters of the heart are involved?"

"They went out for a meal a couple of times a week,

nothing more than that. I think she moved in after a few weeks and then got the ball rolling on the wedding. I know it was a short engagement."

"And how did Jenny react to her father finding another woman and inviting her to move in with them? I'm presuming Jenny lived here alone with her father up until that time?"

"No, Greg, Alvin's son, was around then. Things were fraught, shall we say? Not with Jenny, she accepted Bethany, but Greg detested her. He moved out, or he might have been forced to leave, after a year of sniping and backchatting his father."

"So, would you say he left bearing a grudge?"

"And some. Hey, I see where this is leading. No, don't go there, he would never hurt his father."

"Glad to hear it, however, someone did, and unless we can find out who, there's a killer walking the streets. Who's to say if or when they will strike next?"

Mick placed the bucket he was holding on the floor, wiped his hand clean on his trousers, and then ran it through his greying hair. "When you put it like that, it sounds so cold and merciless, but I don't think Greg could genuinely hurt his father."

"Do you know where he lives now?"

"Somewhere over near Penrith, I think. Alvin never spoke about his son, not after he moved out. I believe Jenny is still in touch with her brother, so it might be worth having a word with her."

"We will, when she's up to speaking with us. What about people Alvin may have fallen out with, anyone coming to mind?"

"Not really, no. Farmers are always falling out with people, but it's generally forgotten about within a day or two. Nothing in particular is coming to mind. Unless… there was a

Land Rover blocking one of the gates the other day. The idiot was off with his camera, taking photos, and we had moved the sheep. They were wandering the roads, causing a traffic jam because the idiot was parked in front of the gates. He showed up eventually, after about an hour or so. Not in the least apologetic, quite the opposite, in fact. Threatened to sue Alvin for not allowing him to park there as, apparently, it's a free country, arsehole. I had to restrain Alvin, he was on the verge of decking the imbecile, and who could blame him? People like that make me sick, no idea what goes on in the hills most days. As long as they're all right, that's all that matters."

"I know the type. And yes, people should be more courteous and never block a farmer's access point. Was he local?"

"I don't think so. Made up some story about working for *Country Life* and said he was taking some shots of the beautiful area. I smelt bullshit from a mile off with that tale."

Sam smiled. "Some people, eh?" She glanced over her shoulder at the farmhouse. She could just make out Bethany standing at one of the windows on the ground floor. "How do you get on with Bethany?"

"She's all right. I tend to keep out of her way most of the time."

"Can you tell me what their relationship was like?"

"I'd describe it as hit and miss most days. This is between you and me, right?"

"Of course." Sam leaned in.

"There were days when I would catch Alvin sitting on a bale of hay, contemplating life."

"Meaning?"

"I don't know, maybe he regretted marrying her, that was my assumption. I might be talking shite, though, because there were other days when he couldn't stop talking about her, you know, praising her."

"Praising her?"

"For doing all the necessary things around the house. Keeping it clean, making wholesome meals every night. Let's say his belly was never empty. That has gone down well with every man I've ever known, to have a woman caring for his every need at home, if you get my drift."

"Are you talking about in the bedroom as well?"

He tapped the side of his nose. "I couldn't possibly comment on that aspect of their relationship."

"Fair enough. Do you know what's going to happen next? With the farm?"

"I'm presuming it will be business as usual until Bethany tells me otherwise. I don't think she's in any fit state to make any rash decisions about anyone's future. She's grieving, she'll need to deal with that first. I'll be here for the family, they know that. I'm gutted about Alvin. Maybe I should have told you that at the beginning of our conversation." He smiled.

"Don't worry. I was guilty of trying to get to the truth quickly. You're not on my suspect list." She peered over her shoulder again to see the curtain twitching.

The same can't be said for Bethany, though. There's something not quite right with that one. But I need the proof to start knocking on her door. It's not practical at this time, not when she's classed as a grieving widow. I think I'll have a word with DCI Armstrong when I get back to the station, see if she's raised a complaint against me.

"Good to know," Mick said. "We had a good working relationship. I'm guessing I'm going to be put upon now, but I don't mind. I'll be willing to help out if I'm needed, in the circumstances."

"It's great that you're willing to go the extra mile for the family. I hope they don't take advantage of you."

"Only time will tell. Is there anything else I can do for you? If not, I really need to get on."

"Not for now. We're going to leave you to it and may pop back to see you if anything crops up during our investigation."

"Feel free. If I think of anything else, can I give you a call?"

Sam removed a card from her pocket and gave it to him.

He shoved it in the front of his overalls.

"Ring me, day or night."

"I'll do that. Sorry you had to feel the wrath of Bethany. That was uncalled for. I suppose we have to make exceptions for folks when they're grieving."

"Easy to do, in the circumstances. Don't worry about me, I have broad shoulders. Take care."

He smiled and continued feeding the pigs. Sam and Bob left the barn and walked back across the farmyard towards the car, Sam's eye drawn to the woman still watching them from the downstairs window.

"I thought we were going to follow him round and ask questions," Bob said. "What changed?"

"One guess," Sam replied. "Let's get in the car. I hate being under the microscope."

"Ah, I'm with you. Mick was right, she shouldn't have had a go at you like that. What a bloody nerve."

"Yeah, let's discuss it in the car or when we get back to the station."

Sam kept one eye on the window until they left the farmyard. "She's freaking me out. I feel out of my comfort zone when dealing with her. I've never felt that way before. Am I being oversensitive?"

"I'm not picking up anything about her, not along the same lines you are. But then I'm not female, nor do I have female intuition running through my veins."

She grinned at her partner, despite the unsettling sensation toying with her nerve endings. "You're not in touch with your feminine side either, by the sound of it."

"So true. What are you going to do about her?"

"Bide my time. I'll drop by and have a word with Armstrong when we get back, see if Bethany's done the deed and put in a complaint or whether she was trying to put the wind up me."

"I bet it's the former."

THEY RETURNED to the station to find DCI Armstrong waiting in Sam's office. Claire had warned her what to expect as they'd arrived.

"He doesn't seem too happy, boss."

"Thanks, Claire. I was expecting him to turn up sooner or later. We're not to be disturbed, okay?"

The team either nodded or raised a thumb.

Sam drew in a breath to steady her nerves and entered her office to find Armstrong sitting in the chair that he had moved, peering out of the window at the views of the hills beyond.

"You have a far better view from here than I have at the rear of the building. Why is that?"

"Umm... I don't have a clue, sir. Can I get you a coffee?"

"No, thanks. I prefer the taste of rich roast, not the crap you have on offer down here."

"Sadly, I don't have a choice, not unless I buy my own rich roast and a proper machine to brew it in. That's beside the point. What can I do for you?"

Sam squeezed past him, the manoeuvre succinctly difficult for each of them. She sat in her usual seat behind the desk.

He cocked an eyebrow and studied her. "I've had a call and wanted to see what you had to say about it."

"Oh, do you want me to guess who from or are you going to tell me?"

"I take it the lady in question, a Mrs Davidson, issued the threat at her property when you visited earlier, is that correct?"

"Yes. In my defence, I was questioning the farmhand in the barn. She crept up behind me, got the wrong end of the stick and ended up jumping down my throat. Both Mick Bartlett and Bob, will corroborate my story."

"I had a feeling that might be the case. You have an exemplary record around here, Sam, don't let your standards drop."

"I have no intention of doing that, sir, it was a genuine mistake. She's a grieving widow, her emotions must be all over the place or…"

"Or? Don't stop there. Is there more to this complaint that I should know about?"

Sam sighed and shrugged. "It's hard to pinpoint. How shall I put this? Ah, yes, let's just say my instincts are on full alert."

"Do you want to run through things with me?"

"If you want. There's really not much to tell as such. It's the impression I'm getting every time I have any kind of interaction with the woman. Yes, we can put it down to her being overwrought and concerned for her family and business after her husband's death, but I'm getting the feeling that there's far more at stake here."

"What are you going to do about it?"

"Keep digging for evidence to back up my assumption. My team and I will be doing that for the rest of the day."

"Are you telling me that you think this woman killed her husband?"

"It's not unheard of. Let's just say my arse is painful right now from sitting on the fence, although I'm erring on the side of her being the murderer. As always, in these types of cases, it's easy to say, but I need the evidence to back up my claim. My suspicions have escalated now that she's rung you to complain about something so insignificant."

"I didn't believe her, not for one second. You do what is necessary and keep me up to date on this one. I know I say that with every case you work on, but this time I truly mean it and, Sam, for goodness sake, watch your back. From what you've told me about her, she seems mighty unstable and capable of doing a lot of damage, either to you personally or to your flourishing career."

"Thanks for believing me, sir. I'm glad you have my back. I've never let you down in the past and don't intend doing it in the future, either."

He rose from his seat and walked towards the door. "Good, ensure that never happens. Ring me if I can be of assistance, and remember what I said, watch your back at all times."

"I will. Thanks again for giving me the benefit of the doubt, sir."

"Always, you're one of my best officers. I refuse to let anyone tarnish your excellent record. They'll have me to deal with if they try. I'll always come down on your side, Sam, umm... within reason of course."

Sam smiled. "That's great to hear, thank you, sir."

Never one for small talk, Armstrong left the office. Sam shook out her arms and swished her head from side to side to relieve the tension in her neck and her shoulders.

What a bitch! Well, you're going to regret coming after me so early into the investigation, Bethany Davidson. All you've managed to do is highlight a need to keep a watchful eye on you and bring you in for questioning, if I need to. Were you the one who fiddled with your husband's tyres last night?

Sam called Bob into her office.

"How did it go?" he asked tentatively.

"He was putty in my hands. Started off stern and abrupt but agreed with me when I revealed how I felt about Mrs Davidson. I've got something going round in my head, Bob, that I want to run past you."

"Whoa, when I'm running on empty? I think we need a coffee, don't you?"

Sam tutted and then nodded. "Go on then, you've twisted my arm."

She made a few notes until he returned with two cups of coffee. "Thanks. Right, get your notebook out and flip it back to what Jenny said about last night for me, would you?"

"I've got it. What are you specifically looking for?"

"If I remember correctly, Jenny said she left the farm last night. Can you confirm that for me?"

"I've got it. That's right, she said she left the house at around six to go to the college. You're not thinking that she was the one who was sneaking around her father's car, are you?"

"No, however, she's admitted that she was out of the way. That would make it possible for *Bethany* to leave the farm without anyone else's knowledge, am I right?"

"It depends if she had access to a vehicle or not."

"Can you check? Did you notice another car parked up in the farmyard today?" Sam struggled to cast her mind back, to visualise the area from earlier.

"I didn't notice. I'll do some digging. What are you saying? That you're now placing her as our chief suspect?"

Sam threw her arms up in the air and leaned back. "I don't know. What do you reckon? She's set the chief on me.

An innocent person wouldn't do that, would they? I believe she's shot herself in the foot with that move."

"Interesting. We didn't really get much from Jenny, did we? Would it be worth visiting the salon where she works? Having a chat with her there, away from bolshy Bethany?"

"The problem with that is, I doubt if she's back at work yet. We only broke the news to her first thing this morning. I know it seems an eternity ago, but it's only been what, six or seven hours?"

"Ah, I'm with you. Then we're up the proverbial creek, aren't we?"

"Not at all. Do the necessary research, then we can check any footage around the area of the pub, see if we can spot her car."

"It's a long shot. Have we got anything else to go on?"

"Not yet, that's why it's imperative to go with what we have, for now."

Bob eased himself out of the chair and took his mug with him. "Leave it with me."

Sam sat there, staring at the door for a few minutes, recapping the events of the day before she turned her attention to the post lying in her in-tray. She started up her computer to check her emails—nothing of importance there. It took her nearly thirty minutes to sift through the post and address anything she regarded as high priority, choosing to leave the rest until either later that day or add it to the to-do pile for the morning. Then she left her office to see what the team had come up with.

"Okay, what have we managed to find out, folks?" Her eye was immediately drawn to her partner who looked her way. "Bob, any luck on the vehicles?"

"Yes, I've got two more cars registered to that address. One belongs to Jenny, and the other is in Bethany's name. Liam and I are examining the ANPR cameras and the CCTV footage surrounding the area of the pub now. Nothing to report so far."

"What about background checks? Am I chancing my arm there, Claire?"

"A bit early yet, boss. I reckon we should have all we need by mid-morning tomorrow. I'll keep chasing my sources."

"If you would. I think we're going to be up against it with this case. Has anyone checked the social media for the family?"

"I had a brief look," Suzanna said.

Sam crossed the room to chat with her. "And? Anything of use there?"

"Jenny is far more active than either her father or her stepmother, so I concentrated on her more than the others."

"Okay, and did you learn anything from her posts?"

"Not really. I'm getting the impression that she tends to spend a lot of her spare time with friends, not at the farm."

"So, she works at the salon and then stays in town with her friends? Is that most nights? Occasionally? What are we talking about here?"

"I'll go over her posts more thoroughly, boss."

Sam smiled and squeezed Suzanna's shoulder and moved around the room. "While we're at it, and not wishing to leave anyone out, can we also see what we can find out about Mick Bartlett? I'm not saying he has anything to do with the murder, but I'd hate to dismiss anyone at this early stage, only for it to bite us in the arse later. It's clear this investigation isn't going to be a clear-cut one, so the more we can pre-empt things the better, right?"

The team agreed with her thought process. Sam crossed the room and filled out the whiteboard that had remained blank due to her lack of time spent at the station. She wrote down the names of the family members and circled Bethany's name several times.

What are you up to, Mrs Davidson?

Deep in thought, Bob snuck up behind and startled her.

"Jesus, give a girl a heart attack, why don't you. What have you found, if anything?"

"Nothing, nothing at all."

"That's disappointing. Is that because there are no cameras in the area?"

"Yep, lack of ANPR and CCTV cameras around the pub and leading up to it."

"I thought as much because of where it's located." Sam pulled at her hair. "Grr... okay, folks, time is getting on now. Why don't we call it a day and start afresh in the morning?"

"It's not like you to finish bang on five, boss," Bob said, stifling a yawn.

"We were both called to the scene at the crack of dawn. My brain is fried, and we're not getting anywhere, not from what I can tell. Feel free to put in the extra hours, don't let me stop you."

"Err... no. I'm going to listen to my mother's advice here and never look a gift horse in the mouth."

"Quite right. I have to stop off at the supermarket on the way home, pick up a present for Doreen. See you in the morning, folks." Sam breezed into her office, switched off the computer, tidied up a few stray papers on her desk and collected her jacket. When she returned to the incident room, the rest of the team, except for Bob, had left for the day. "You and me against the world as usual, partner."

"Looks that way. Do you have any plans for this evening?"

"Nope. I envisage a nice bottle of wine with dinner and feet up in front of a romcom, I hope. What about you?"

"Similar, I bet my missus has other ideas, though. Abigail has made it her mission to pick fault in the house and give me a list of jobs that need doing. She's either nesting or thinking of putting the house on the market, I'm not sure which."

Sam sniggered. "Poor you. Either of those options wouldn't be good news to me."

"Yeah, I'm thinking along the same lines. I'm getting too old to move house again."

"Umm... and you're not too old to become a father again, is that what you're saying?"

"Good heavens, I'd die if that were the case." He shuddered and retched.

"You crack me up. Right, I'm off. Are you fit to leave?"

"Yep, ready to drop. Not sure if I'll be fit for anything else by the time I get home, but I'm sure Abigail will have a list the length of my arm she wants completing by bedtime, providing I don't fall asleep whilst eating my dinner."

"I'm sure you'll survive. You could always try speaking up for yourself."

His eyes widened, and his head jutted forward. "Have you met my wife?"

Sam laughed and left the office. Bob followed her out of the room once he'd switched the computers and lights off.

They said farewell at the cars, and Sam rang Rhys on the way to the supermarket.

"Hey, I'm stopping off at the shop. Do we need anything urgent? Please don't give me a list of necessities, I'm shattered."

"Hey, come straight home then. I can get what we need to top up the cupboards during my lunch hour tomorrow."

"No, it's fine. I need to pop in and pick up something for Doreen. Anything we need?" she repeated.

"Maybe some milk, that's all. You should have given me a ring earlier; I could have popped next door to the chocolate shop. Silly me, if I'd thought about it, I could have bought Doreen a gift from there, sorry."

"Not to worry. I'll be home soon, love you."

"Love you, too. Don't worry, dinner is already on the go, I finished early today. Want me to take the dogs out now, or would you rather we do it together, later? Bearing in mind you've had a really long day."

"You're a treasure, would you mind? I'm dead on my feet as it is."

"No problem. Don't fret when you get back and find us all missing."

"I won't. I'll drop in on Doreen and have a cuppa with her, if that's all right with you?"

"Go for it. See you later."

Sam ended the call and got on the road. Morrisons was just around the corner, the nearest supermarket to the station, so she headed over there. The car park was heaving which would only mean one thing—the shop would be full to the brim with people loitering in the aisles. She detested food shopping at the best of times and groaned frequently as shoppers got in the way of her sprinting around the shopfloor in search of the essentials she needed. The queue at the tills was horrendous, forcing her to use the detestable self-service checkout, yet another bugbear of hers.

With a box of chocolates and a bunch of flowers, not forgetting a four-pint of milk tucked in her arms, she darted back to the car and drove home. Doreen, bless her, was sitting at the window, the glow from the lamp forming a shadow on the curtains behind her. Sam blew her a kiss, collected her goodies from the passenger seat and locked up the car, then she let herself into Doreen's with the key her neighbour had given her.

She entered the living room and asked, "All right to let myself in?"

"Of course it is. How are you, dear? Rhys said you were

up and out of the door before dawn broke this morning. You've had an extremely long day to contend with."

Sam pecked Doreen on the cheek and shoved the bunch of flowers and the box of Dairy Milk in her hands before her neighbour had a chance to complain. "Here you go. Rhys said you'd had a fall. How are you?"

"You are naughty. They're appreciated, but you should save your money, not spend it on me. I've told you that dozens of times, haven't I?"

"You have, and I always ignore you. Seriously, Doreen, how are you?"

"I'm fine. Tweaked my ankle. It hurts more when I'm resting it. I need to keep active, and don't you dare make other arrangements for Sonny, it's he who's keeping me going. It won't mend if I sit around here all day with my feet up, in spite of what you might think. I know what's best for my body."

Sam laughed. "Have you finished? Can I get a word in now?"

Doreen hunched her shoulders up to her ears and giggled. "Consider me told. Okay, you can speak now."

"Thank you. You know I feel bad putting on you, day in and day out. I'm aware of what a handful Boy Wonder can be at times..."

"Nonsense. Don't you dare take the privilege of caring for him away from me. I don't think I would ever forgive you, Sam."

She sighed. "Doreen, I'm thinking of your well-being. Let's face it, you're not getting any younger, neither of us is. It's a huge responsibility I'm putting on your shoulders every day."

"You're not. Don't be so absurd. Please, I'll be fine. Do you want me to prove it to you? I will if you want me to." Doreen tried to stand, but her ankle gave way, and she flopped back into her seat. She slapped her knee and cursed under her breath, and a trail of tears dripped onto her cheek.

Sam leaned forward and hugged her. "You need time for it to heal. Let me ask Vernon to look after Sonny for the next day or two. Please?" She pulled away from her dear friend. "You're breaking my heart, dearest lady. I'm worried about you, can't you see that?"

"I… I feel useless most of the time. Caring for Sonny every day gives me a purpose in this life. Something to live for. Surely you can see that, can't you?"

Sam knelt on the floor beside Doreen and grasped both of her hands in her own. "Your ankle is weak, you can barely stand on it. Just give it a rest for a few days. Let me give my brother-in-law a call, see if he'll dog sit for a while, just until you're able to walk on it better. What do you say?"

"And there's no point in me arguing with you, is there?"

"No, I'm adamant about this. I'm doing what's best for you, special lady."

Doreen sniffled, and Sam plucked a tissue from the box on the coffee table beside her. "Please don't fall out with me about this."

"Here, wipe your nose and dry your eyes, not necessarily in that order."

Sam smiled, but Doreen appeared to be thoroughly dejected, and Sam's heart broke into a gazillion pieces. Tears pricked, and she swallowed down the lump that swelled in her throat.

"I could *never* fall out with you," Sam said. "How could you even think that of me? You've been so kind to me since I moved in."

"You're like a daughter to me, Sam. I know I've never told you that before, but since your mother passed away… I'm sorry, please don't cry. I shouldn't have brought her into the conversation."

Sam smiled and wiped her tears away. "Mum is in a better place; this isn't about her. I feel the same way about you. You've been amazing to all of us, but there are days when guilt comes knocking because I feel I'm taking advantage of you."

"You're not. I've never felt that way about our arrangement. What else am I going to do all day? Sit in the chair, watching mind-numbing daytime TV? Sonny gives me more than a reason to live. When you're not around, he sits there, staring at me, waiting for me to give him permission to get up on the couch for a cuddle."

"He's adorable, and I appreciate he thinks the world of you. Every morning he waits by the front door, eager to come and see you, while I put on my shoes. I'm not denying that you'll both miss each other's company. What I'm more concerned about is if he trips you up and causes damage to your other ankle. Where would you be then?"

Doreen heaved out a sigh. "I know you're talking a lot of sense and Sonny is your dog and you have a right to be concerned about him, but…"

"I know, you'd be lost without him. Why don't we see how you are in the morning and reassess the situation then? In the meantime, I'll put Vernon on alert, how's that?"

"If you think that would be for the best."

Sam wasn't convinced that Doreen felt the option was a good one. "Have you eaten a main meal today yet?"

Doreen slowly shook her head. "I'll get something out of the freezer if I'm hungry later. I haven't got much of an appetite."

"I've got a better idea. Why don't you come and spend the evening with us? Have a meal and a nice chat. We haven't done that in a while, have we?"

"There's really no need. You and Rhys will be wanting and needing to unwind after your hard day at work. The last thing you want is an old woman with a messed-up ankle getting in your way."

"Nonsense. Come on, give me a hand. It's dry out, so there's no need for you to put your shoes on. Come in your slippers."

Doreen beamed. "It would be nice to have some human company for a couple of hours."

"Right, let's get you up on your feet then."

With some effort, Sam managed to get Doreen to the front door.

"Wait, I think the back door might be unlocked. Would you mind checking that for me?"

Sam left Doreen clinging to the bannisters for support and rushed into the kitchen. She locked the back door and inspected the sink to see if there were any dishes or cups in there. It was empty. Which probably meant that Doreen hadn't had anything to eat or drink all day.

Sam returned to the hallway and removed Doreen's coat from the hook by the door. "We'll slip this around your shoulders. I've just had a thought, how are you going to make it upstairs to bed tonight?"

Doreen batted her question away with her frail hand. "I'll sort that out later, don't worry about me."

"We'll see. Come on, I'm starving. You must be, too, it's way past your teatime, isn't it?"

"No comment," Doreen said with a smile.

Rhys was a few feet away from the front door, returning from his walk with the dogs. He let them off their leads and opened the gate for them, then came back to assist Sam and Doreen.

"Everything all right?" he asked, concerned.

Sam nodded and smiled. "Yes, Doreen has agreed to join us for dinner."

"Oh, great stuff. Let me help."

"We're fine. You get the dogs inside. Put them in the kitchen so they don't hinder us, if you wouldn't mind."

Doreen managed to hobble up the short path, but when it came to setting foot into the house it was a different story, until Rhys lent a hand.

"You are struggling, dear friend, aren't you?" he said.

"Just a touch. I'm sorry to be a nuisance to you both."

"You're not," Sam chided. "I think I have an ankle support upstairs. I'll go and fetch that once we have you settled. Why don't you take a seat in the lounge while we cobble a meal together?"

"Sounds wonderful, if you're sure," Doreen replied, a note of relief in her tone.

They shuffled through the cottage's narrow doorway and into the lounge. After lowering Doreen onto the sofa, Rhys switched on the news.

"Do you want a drink, Doreen? Fancy a glass of wine for a change?"

Doreen's cheeks flushed. "Now you're spoiling me."

"That's the plan. Red or white?"

"A nice glass of red for me, thank you, Rhys."

Sam placed a blanket over Doreen's lap and checked the radiator was turned up high then left the room. "What are we going to have for dinner?" she whispered, once they were alone in the kitchen.

"Let me see what we've got in the freezer that will stretch to three of us. I can put the chicken casserole I've already knocked up on hold," Rhys said. "You pour the wine, for all of us, I think we're going to need it. What sort of things does she eat?"

"I don't know. Sorry to mess you around. Is there a bolognaise in there?"

"I think there is. Why don't you go and ask her? You can take her drink in at the same time."

Sam quickly poured Doreen a drink and took it into the lounge. "Here you go, young lady, enjoy. Do you like spaghetti bolognaise?"

"I love it. Although, I haven't had it for a while because I end up in a mess with the spaghetti."

"Do you want some pasta shells instead?"

"Now why didn't I think of that? Sounds like a bright idea to me, if I'm not putting you to any trouble, dear."

"You're not, it's already made. It won't be long. Will you be all right to eat it in here?"

"Suits me fine. Thank you again, Sam."

"Nonsense. After all you do for us, this is nothing in comparison. We won't be long."

She returned to the kitchen and let out a relieved sigh. "She loves it but would prefer pasta shells."

"Phew! Sounds good to me. Can you get those sorted? I'll defrost the sauce and grate some cheese to go on top."

"Take two sauces out, one might not be enough for all three of us."

CHAPTER 4

Fifteen minutes later, and they were all tucking into their evening meal. Doreen's eyes filled up with tears as she was eating, enough to warrant Sam asking her if everything was okay.

"What's wrong, is it your ankle?"

"No, it's just me being silly. I'm blown away by your kindness. You truly are the best people I know."

Sam smiled. "We're only repaying the favour, Doreen. How's your dinner?"

"It's divine. I used to make this all the time. I don't tend to bother now that I'm on my own."

"I can always give you a portion or two the next time I'm making a batch, it's no bother."

"That'd be lovely, Sam."

After they'd finished the meal, Sam dashed upstairs to search for her ankle support. She found it in the last drawer she checked. "Finally." She ensured it was clean and took it downstairs to see if it was a comfortable fit for Doreen. They were about the same size, so odds were that it would.

"Oh my, that feels tight but such a relief." Doreen twisted

her ankle around without wincing. "You're a miracle worker, Sam."

She laughed. "I don't think so. They are brilliant, when they work. Do you want to try walking on it?"

Sam and Rhys helped Doreen to her feet. She shrugged them off once she was standing and paraded around the room as if twenty years had been lifted from her shoulders. "Goodness me, the change is remarkable. Right, on that note, and while I'm up on my feet again, I'm going to let you get on with your evening together."

"Don't be silly, spend some more time with us. We have salted caramel ice cream for pudding."

"Umm… well, if that's okay with you? I don't want to get in the way and become a nuisance."

"You're not and never could be."

"I'll get the ice cream," Rhys announced and left the room.

Sam eased Doreen back into her seat. "I wouldn't have it on for any longer than a couple of hours at a time, but definitely use it if you're intending to walk around the house or if you venture into the garden with this one for a game of fetch." She ruffled Sonny's head, and he licked her hand and then her face. "Get out of it, you little tyke."

"He's adorable. He has a sweet, lovable soul. Mind you, I'm not surprised, he takes after his mum on that score."

"Do you know his mother?" Sam winked.

"I meant you. You're truly one in a million. Up at five this morning and still on the go now, caring for me as if it were second nature to you."

"It's no hardship on my part, I can assure you. You're always welcome to join us in the evening, if only to share a meal with us, you know that, don't you?"

"Thank you." Doreen peered over her shoulder then leaned in and whispered, "He's a gazillion times better than that other one, Chris."

Sam's cheeks flushed. "I know. I fell on my feet when I met him at the park."

"Sorry? Is that where you met?"

"Yes, he had Benji back then. He was there walking his dog the same time I was there with Sonny. We struck up a conversation and appeared to hit it off right away. He'd not long moved to the area and started up his new practice."

"And you were with Chris at the time, as I recall, going through that rough patch."

"That's right. I've never felt attracted to anyone else before, not while I was married. I still feel a little guilty about that now and again."

"You shouldn't. You two were meant to be together, I mean you and Rhys. Chris never treated you right. Wasn't he seeing other people behind your back?"

"Yes, that solicitor. Anyway, it's all in the past now."

"You couldn't have chosen a better man to share your life with going forward, Sam. Have you set a date for the wedding yet?"

"We're trying to, but what with losing mum, making any kind of wedding arrangements was put on hold."

"I can understand that, but life goes on, love. Your mother is still around you. She'll be up there, cheering you on every step of the way. It might be what your family needs to get over the heartbreak of losing her. How is your father coping?"

"I need to check in with him, so far so good, although he has days when he's a bit quiet on the phone. Crystal is keeping a watchful eye on him, but I still need to step up to the plate and do my part as well."

"Hard to do that when you have twelve- or fourteen-hour shifts to contend with, sweetie."

"I know. It keeps me out of mischief, though, doesn't it?"

"Knock, knock, all right to come in?" Rhys entered, carrying a tray with three large bowls of ice cream.

"Were your ears burning?" Sam asked.

"No, why?" He handed the desserts around and sat on the end of the sofa.

"Doreen has been singing your praises."

"Ah, why thank you, dear lady. I do my best."

"What Sam hasn't told you is that I also asked when you were going to tie the knot."

Sam nearly choked on her ice cream, and Rhys chuckled.

"Maybe you can help me persuade Sam to choose a date?"

Doreen grinned and prepared a spoonful of ice cream. "With pleasure."

"Oh crikey, I sense I'm being ganged up on here. Help me, boys." She hugged Sonny and Jasper who had their eyes on her dessert when she placed it on the floor and pulled them in for a cuddle.

"Cupboard love, they're only after your ice cream." Rhys laughed.

"And who could blame them? It's delicious," Doreen agreed.

Doreen ended up staying with them for another hour, then Sam accompanied her back home, pleased to see the ankle support appeared to be working its magic.

She pecked Doreen on the cheek. "Are you sure you don't want me to take you upstairs before I leave?"

"I'm sure. I've taken up enough of your time this evening. This support is fantastic. Go and enjoy the rest of your evening, and Sam, thank you, with all my heart."

"The pleasure was all ours. We'll have to do it more often."

"You're an angel in disguise, don't ever let anyone tell you otherwise."

They shared a hug, and Sam closed the door behind her.

She returned to the house and locked up for the evening. Rhys was in the kitchen doing the dishes.

"Hey, I'll do that."

"We'll do it together. That was a lovely evening. I think Doreen enjoyed herself."

"I've left her teary-eyed next door. She had a blast. Thank you for being so kind to her."

Rhys stopped wiping the side down next to the sink and faced her. "Why wouldn't I be? After all she does for us."

"Not every bloke would think that way."

"You're talking about Chris, aren't you?"

"Yep. He would have sat in the corner all night, his arms crossed and his lips taut, refusing to interact with us."

"Really? That would have been plain ignorant of him."

"Yep, he was that at times." She continued to dry the dishes, her thoughts still with Doreen until she neared the end of her chores when her father's image floated into her mind. "I need to give Dad a call."

"Go on, it's getting late. I can finish this off and see to the dogs."

She handed him the tea towel and leaned in for a kiss. "I truly don't know what I would do without you by my side."

"Ditto. We make a great team, Sam. Maybe Doreen is right, perhaps we should concentrate on our future and think about setting a date?"

"We could do it over the weekend if you're up to it?"

"What, get married?"

"I… umm… we couldn't possibly organise things that quickly."

"I was joking."

"Oh, I see. Anytime is fine by me."

They shared a long, lingering kiss that took her breath away.

"I won't be long."

"Take your time. Send your dad my regards."

"I will." She left him to finish clearing up the kitchen and went back into the lounge. "Hello, Dad, how are you?"

"Sorry, who is this?"

Sam laughed. "Ouch, that was like a dagger to the heart."

Her father snorted. "Sorry, I couldn't resist it. How are you both?"

"I asked first."

"I'm fine. Good days mixed in with a few bad ones here and there. It hits me when I least expect it to, like during the night. I woke up to find myself crying, images of your mother being laid to rest uppermost in my mind."

"Oh, Dad. You should have rung me."

"Don't be so absurd, this was two-fifteen in the morning. You'd throttle me if I ever did that to you."

"I wouldn't. I get calls during the night all the time," Sam fibbed.

"Hmm… you're just saying that."

"All right, perhaps that was a half-truth. The rate I dish out my business cards to victims' families, I'm surprised I don't get bombarded week in, week out."

"You need to stop doing that. There are lots of weirdos walking the streets these days."

She sniggered. "Don't I know it? It's not my personal number, Dad, it's the mobile I use for work."

"Ah, that's different. Have you heard from your sister lately?"

"No, I need to give her a call. Not tonight, though, I've been at work since around five-thirty."

"Good heavens, what the heck are you doing ringing me then? You should be winding down for the evening, getting ready for bed."

She explained the situation with Doreen. "We're fine. She's amazing the way she copes on her own."

"Needs must. Tell her to give me a call if she ever gets lonely."

"That's kind of you, Dad. I'll pass the message on. What have you been up to lately?"

"I've started a little job, it's not paid."

"A volunteer? Where?"

"Yes, at the local dog shelter."

"That's fantastic. Are you thinking of getting a four-legged companion?" Sam said. She had an inkling what was going through his mind.

"I might. I have my eye on a little Jack Russell called Monty. His family gave him up when a new baby came on the scene. He's nearly eight, poor old soul."

"You should go for it; he sounds as if he needs a caring home to see out the rest of his days."

"We're taking it slowly. He has an issue with trusting men. We think his previous owner abused him."

"Bless him. If anyone can turn him around and show him some love, it's you, Dad."

"We'll see. Your mother and I often spoke about getting a dog when we retired, we just never got around to taking the plunge."

"I'm glad you've given up work. I thought it might be too soon for you."

"Losing your mother at her age was an eye-opener for me. What's the point in building up a pension pot when you pop your clogs before you get a chance to enjoy it?"

"Exactly. You always talked about getting a campervan, too, and travelling the length and breadth of the UK, with a little doggy by your side. That would be amazing for you."

He fell silent, and Sam wondered if she'd said the wrong thing.

"Do you know what? You're right. I could sell this place, get something smaller and travel the UK with a furry friend.

That would give me something to look forward to, wouldn't it?"

"There you go. That and a wedding."

He gasped. "Wedding? Yours?"

"Yes, we've decided to sit down at the weekend to choose a date."

"It's about time. Your mother would be so proud of you, darling."

"I know and I've got the added bonus of having a sister who owns a bridal boutique."

"She'll be thrilled if you have one of her dresses. You won't go overboard and get into debt for it, though, love, promise me that?"

"We won't, it'll be something simple at the registry office."

Rhys entered the lounge with Sonny and Jasper. Sam patted the seat beside her for Rhys to snuggle up.

"I know you've got your head screwed on and that bastard saddled you with all those debts before he… took his own miserable life. Shame on him, spoiling your future like that."

"No point dwelling on it, Dad. I'm coping, don't worry about me."

"You have a good man beside you now, Sam. He'll be a welcome addition to the family. Your sister has Vernon, and you have an excellent partner in Rhys. That's all a proud dad could wish for."

"You, soppy old fool. Your girls done good, eh?"

"You certainly have, my dear. Right, I have a cup of hot chocolate going cold here. Was there anything else you wanted to share with me?"

"No, just checking in. Give me a shout if you need to chat, I mean it."

"I know, darling. Love you. Ring me once you've set a date."

"Why don't you come for dinner on Sunday?"

Rhys nodded beside her, and she squeezed his hand in appreciation.

"I might take you up on that. I'll have to check my diary first."

They all laughed.

"Nutter. Speak soon. Good luck with Monty."

They blew each other a kiss, and she ended the call.

"Monty? Am I missing something?" Rhys handed her a glass of wine, her second of the evening.

"Dad's volunteering at a dog shelter and has become attached to a Jack Russell called Monty."

"He should go for it. He'd love a cute companion to keep him occupied."

"Exactly what I said. He's also talking about selling up, downsizing and buying a campervan."

"Wow, he's not letting the grass grow under his feet, is he? Good for him. Your mum wouldn't want to think of him sitting at home being depressed all day."

"That's what I told him."

"And you told him about fixing a date at the weekend, too, I gather?"

"I did. He said he woke up during the night crying and couldn't get back to sleep. I wanted to give him something to look forward to. I also asked him over for Sunday lunch. You don't mind, do you?"

"Nope. The more the merrier. Why don't you ask Crystal and Vernon to come along as well? And we'll drag Doreen in to join us, whether she wants to or not."

"Gosh, that would be a houseful. Are you sure?"

"Yep, hopefully we'll have something special to celebrate by then, won't we?"

"Fingers crossed. Oh, yes, also, I've booked a table for

Saturday night at a pub I discovered today, during the investigation."

"How exciting. I love finding new places to eat. I predict we have a busy weekend ahead of us." He chinked his glass against hers.

"Provided the investigation doesn't take over and spoil our arrangements."

"Is that likely?" he asked.

"I'm not sure. I hope not."

"You haven't had a chance to tell me about it. Do you want to discuss it?"

"Not really. I want to spend time with you, not going over work."

He grinned and said, "We could always take our wine up to bed with us."

"Now you're talking."

They shared another kiss, and he touched the tip of her nose with his finger.

"You're a special lady, Sam."

"You're not so bad yourself. Like you said earlier, we make a dream team. If I have one regret in this life it's…" She paused as a lump formed in her throat.

"Go on," he whispered.

"That I didn't meet you sooner. Actually, I have two."

"What's that?"

"That Mum didn't live to see us exchange our vows. She would have loved that."

"She'll be there with us on the day. I have no doubt about it."

"I hope so. I think it's going to be a very special day indeed."

CHAPTER 5

The next day consisted of putting out the press conference and more of the same which left the team feeling frustrated that they were constantly going round and round in circles. Sam tried to speak to Jenny alone, but as she wasn't back at work yet, she came up against a brick wall. Every time Sam rang the young woman's mobile it was diverted to her answerphone. She refused to leave a message, not when she was desperate to talk to Jenny in person, and Sam felt there was no point in showing up at the farm, demanding to speak to her out of Bethany's earshot as she was cautious about raising the older woman's suspicions at this stage of the investigation.

Infuriatingly, over the last few days, they had encountered a countywide blip on the banking systems, so the team were unable to collect the normal background information they could usually lay their hands on during the early days of a case.

So, the team did their best with the evidence they had to hand. It wasn't until late afternoon that Sam checked her emails and found the PM report had arrived for the victim,

Alvin Davidson. She scan read it with interest and paused close to the end where Des had written there was a fracture at the back of the victim's skull.

So, Des had deduced correctly what had happened at the scene. It's looking likely that the murder was premeditated after all, what with the person we saw messing around with the tyres. Was that you, Bethany Davidson? Without the bloody evidence I need to come after you, I'm powerless to act upon my suspicions. DCI Armstrong has already warned me to be careful and to watch my back. Lodging a complaint is working in your favour so far, but it won't always be the case, not if I have my way.

A knock on the door interrupted her internal assessment of the situation. "Come in."

Bob poked his head into the room. "It's only me. Just checking you're still alive in here and haven't been overwhelmed by paperwork."

"I'm still going strong, there's no need for you to worry on that score. I've received the PM for Davidson. Here, take a look." She passed him the report that she had printed off.

He read it thoroughly. Bob wasn't the quickest of readers. Sam drummed her fingers on the desk.

"Do you mind?" he said. "How do you expect me to concentrate?"

"Sorry, habit. You really need to learn how to scan read important documents."

He glanced up and raised an eyebrow. "And then what? Sit back while you chew my nuts off for missing vital information?"

Sam struggled to suppress the giggle threatening to emerge.

"Oh shit, I've just realised what I said. Ignore me."

"Oh, do I have to? You brighten up my day, most of the time, with your frequent faux pas."

"You really know how to make a partner feel good

about themselves," he complained and continued reading the report. "Heck, I suppose I've just got to the crucial part."

"The possible whack on the head?"

"Yep."

"What do you think we should do about the information?" Sam asked, testing him. It was something she did now and again but not as often as she should.

He stared at her and shrugged. "I guess we're going to have to sit back for a while. The lack of evidence is going to prevent us from talking with Bethany, if that's who you suspect to be behind his murder."

"Yeah, it's getting late now. I'm going to take the report home with me and consider what to do for the best. It's not in me to sit back and do nothing about this, but as things stand, our hands are tied until something concrete comes our way. Time is getting on, it's been another long, drawn-out, frustrating day with the system working against us. Hopefully that will be sorted in the morning, and we can get back to trying to solve this case."

"I suppose there's one thing we need to be grateful for."

Sam inclined her head. "And that is?"

"That we're only dealing with the one murder so far. You know what it's like most weeks around here, they're like buses. They don't usually stop at just one body showing up, do they?"

Sam nodded and smiled. "Many a true word spoken in jest, partner."

"Who's jesting? I was being serious. I reckon over the last couple of years we've had to deal with more serial killers than I've had Pot Noodles, and yes, I've had my fair share of them."

"Christ, I haven't had one of those since I was a kid."

"They're not as good as they used to be. Saying that, I bet

my taste buds have improved over time, so who knows if they've changed the recipe or not?"

"Anyway, let's call it a day and hope for a brighter one tomorrow."

He raised his thumb and walked out of the office.

Sam stared out of the window at the darkness that had descended without her even realising. "Where the bloody hell has the day gone? And we have FA to show for it." She shrugged and switched off her computer, then collected her coat and handbag on her way out. "Goodnight, folks. Sorry today has been a waste of time and out of our control. Let's hope for a different outcome in the morning. Go home and get some rest."

The team filed past her. Sam could tell some of them were low after the day they'd had. Try as she might, she failed to find the words to keep their spirits up, which was a first for her.

"Are you all right?" Bob said, once they were alone. He whizzed around the room, checking all the computers and other equipment were turned off.

"Yeah, I feel for the team. I think this must be the most unproductive day we've ever experienced during an investigation. I don't have to be a genius to see just how much it has affected everyone."

"True, but if it's out of our hands, then there's little either you or I can do about it."

"I know. Come on, let's get out of here. Any plans for this evening?"

"More DIY, I suppose, which is a bugger because I was hoping to go to the pub and watch the football tonight."

Sam rolled her eyes. "God, no thanks. Football is much like your Pot Noodles, not like it used to be. I remember spending most of my time watching my dad's reaction during a match; it used to be hilarious. It's definitely not the same these days. Even he says the players are overpaid wimps."

Bob laughed. "He's probably right. Yeah, there aren't many Terry Butcher types who would request bandaging up a head wound and get on with a game, rather than sit it out on the subs' bench."

"I doubt they're allowed to do it nowadays, due to health and safety reasons. The world has gone nuts."

"I agree, and don't get me started on all things PC, or not as the case may be."

"Yep, that's probably a subject we should steer clear of for now."

They wound their way down the stairs and out into the chilly evening air.

Sam shivered. "Feels like snow. That's all we need."

"I suppose it's to be expected in January. Drive carefully."

"I will. Enjoy your DIY projects, if Abigail has any lined up for you."

Bob groaned and got in his car.

Sam watched him drive away and then opened her door and slid behind the steering wheel. She drove out of the car park and took a left. As usual, she rang Rhys on the way. "Hey, I've just left the station. Do we need anything from the supermarket?"

"No, I did a shop at lunchtime. Just come home."

"I shouldn't be too long." She ended the call. The next thing she knew, her car was being shunted from behind, not once but twice. She looked in her rear-view mirror, but it was too dark to make out the driver. Thinking on her feet, she switched on her blues and twos, and the car behind her veered off the road and up one of the side streets. Sam knew the likelihood of finding the vehicle in the pitch-black was virtually non-existent, so she didn't bother turning around. However, she turned off her siren and lights and pulled over to catch her breath for a moment or two.

What the fuck was that all about? It couldn't have been, could it? She wouldn't dare, would she? Am I guilty of doing her an injustice?

Sam shook her head to rid herself of such thoughts. It was far too dark to tell who the driver was, and just plucking Bethany's name out of the air... well, even to her, it just didn't feel right. Again, she needed the vital proof to pin this attack on her.

I'll take my car to the lab in the morning, see if they can find any evidence I can use against someone in the future before I take it to the garage to get it repaired.

She shook out her arms, ensured all the doors were locked and continued on her journey. She debated whether to tell Rhys or not and, in the end, decided against it. The last thing she wanted was to get him riled up and questioning the safety of her role.

Sam went to bed that night, distracted, her thoughts going over the incident, so much that it kept her awake for hours. Sonny slept beside her until three a.m. She kept her hand out of the bed, stroking him, needing to feel him close for reassurance.

Unable to sleep, she got up at six to let the dogs out. Rhys stirred. She kissed him and told him to go back to sleep. Sam made herself a coffee, leaned against the doorframe and watched the dogs sniff around the garden and do their business. Sleep had evaded her, she'd barely managed to get a couple of hours. That meant the day ahead was going to be as long, if not longer, than the day before, something she was dreading.

"Jasper, Sonny, come in now."

The dogs came after a final sniff and quick wee up one of the roses she'd planted in her mother's honour, but she didn't tell them off. What would have been the point? They wouldn't have understood.

AT EIGHT-FIFTEEN, Sam paid a visit to the lab on her way to work.

One of the techs had a look at the damage caused to her rear bumper and said, "It's not too bad, it could have been a lot worse."

"If I hadn't put my lights and siren on, I think it would've been. Can you take some samples, or do what you need to do to see if you can match any paintwork to the other vehicle?"

"Leave it with me for ten minutes or so. It's cold out here, why don't you get yourself a coffee from the vending machine in the reception area?"

"Good idea. I could do with some caffeine flowing through my veins." She nipped inside the building and selected the flat white option on the machine, only for an alarm to go off, informing her that option wasn't available. She opted for a normal white with one sugar instead.

It was eight-thirty, so she decided to give Bob a call while she waited. "Hey, it's me. Where are you?"

"I've just got in the car, pulling out of my drive now. What's up?"

"I might be a few minutes late, just wanted to give you the heads-up."

"Is something wrong, Sam?"

"Not really. I'm at the lab. Someone tried to run me off the road last night... umm... maybe that was a slight exaggeration on my part."

"Either they did or they didn't, which is it?"

"Someone rear-ended me a couple of times."

"They what? I'm coming over to be with you."

"No, I'm fine, don't make a fuss. I'm getting my car seen to by the tech team before I take it to the garage."

"Good thinking. Did you see who did it?"

"Nope, it was too dark. As soon as I put the blues and twos on, they darted down a side street."

"Do you think they came after you intentionally or were they chancing their luck?"

"I don't know, Bob, you tell me. Sorry, I didn't mean to snap. I've hardly slept a wink all night."

"You don't have to apologise. I appreciate how worked up you must be about this. Were you physically hurt, Sam?"

"No, not in the slightest. Mentally scarred a little, maybe."

"I'm not surprised. Can you tell me where it happened? I'll get cracking on any cameras in the area."

"I was on the A66, about five minutes, if that, from the station. I didn't notice the car following me before it shunted me up the jacksy."

"Okay, leave it with me. How long are you going to be?"

"Another ten minutes here and however long it takes me to drive to the station. I'm just having a coffee to pass the time."

"I'll see you in about half an hour. Take care."

"Thanks, Bob. See you later."

Sam felt crestfallen when she ended the call. She hated being out of her comfort zone with dozens of questions circulating her mind. Was the accident intentional? Did the fact that she had drawn attention to herself scare the driver off? Or was their aim to bump her a few times, just enough to scare the crap out of her? Did they know she was a copper? Or did they see a woman on her own and just want to put the wind up her?

The door opened, and in walked Des. "Hey, what are you doing here? Did we have an early appointment? Has something happened? This is unusual for you, Sam."

"If you'll let me get a word in, I'll tell you."

He leaned against the wall and smirked. "Sorry, you know me, eager to get on with my working day."

"I am, too. I had to stop off on my way to work. One of your guys is taking samples from my rear bumper. Someone, in their infinite wisdom, saw fit to ram me up the arse last night a couple of times. Er... not me personally, I meant my car."

"Shit. Who was it, do you know?"

"I didn't see them. It was too dark to even make out what car it was, let alone who was driving it."

"Are you okay? Any cuts or bruises?"

"A bit shaken up, but nothing more than that."

The tech who had been dealing with Sam's car entered the reception area. "All done. I've managed to get samples of a dark car from the dents in the bumper."

"That's great news. Where do we go from here?" Sam asked, fearing what the answer was going to be.

"All you need now is to find the culprit, and we'll do the necessary with their vehicle to see if it's a match," Des filled in for her.

"Geez... thanks. Simple, right?"

Des shrugged. "I'm sure a savvy detective like you won't have a problem finding the perpetrator, Sam. I need to fly, I have a body I need to cut open first thing before I get inundated, which is the norm around here."

"I'll be in touch soon."

"You do that," he flung over his shoulder.

"Thanks for taking the samples for me. I appreciate it."

"Sorry the news couldn't be better. At least we'll have something on file if you come up with a vehicle to match it against."

"That's one positive. Have a good day." Sam threw the remains of her coffee in the bin and left the building.

She drove to the station, constantly checking her rear-view mirror. *Is this what my life will consist of now? Not trusting the drivers around me, in case I get attacked again?*

She pulled up at the station and parked in her allotted space.

In reception, the desk sergeant, Nick Travis, welcomed her with a frown and a smile. "Morning, ma'am. Everything okay? It's not like you to be late, not that I'm judging you."

Sam returned the smile. "I had to stop off en route. Everything is hunky-dory, Nick. Eager to get down to business and see what the day holds for me and my team."

"I hope it's a good one."

"I'll second that."

Bob was pacing the floor when she arrived.

"What's going on?" Sam asked.

"Nothing, I was clock-watching and thought you'd be here sooner. The closer it got to nine the more apprehensive…"

"I'm fine. Don't go OTT about this, Bob. Don't make me regret telling you. That's the reason I didn't tell Rhys last night."

"What? Are you kidding me? He doesn't know?"

"That's right, and I have no intention of telling him either."

"Holy crap, I've heard it all now. What did the lab say?"

"A dark car hit me. All I have to do is find the suspect and test their vehicle against the scratches made on mine, and bingo bongo, that's another criminal behind bars."

"As easy as that, eh?" Bob finally cracked a smile. "Do you want a coffee?"

"Not for me. I'll see what's turned up in my office overnight and be with you in a while. Is the system up and running again?"

"Yep, all good. I'm about to go over the CCTV footage from your little spat last night."

"Okay, don't waste too much time on it. I'd rather concentrate all our efforts on the investigation."

"What if there's a link? It could be the evidence we're searching for to bring Bethany in for questioning."

Sam nodded. "Makes sense. Okay, let me know what you come up with."

It was mid-morning when things took a turn for the worse. Sam was just about to leave her office when her phone rang.

It was Nick on reception. "Sorry to trouble you, ma'am, but I've just taken a call and I thought you should know about it."

"I'm listening, Nick. Who was it?"

"A very upset young lady. She told me her husband had spoken to you a few days ago. She found one of your business cards and wanted to call you but was too afraid to contact you directly."

"Does this lady have a name?"

"Mrs Tara Bartlett."

Sam gulped. "And her husband is Mick Bartlett?"

"Correct. She's just reported him missing."

Sam shot out of her chair and hitched her jacket on. "Okay, I'll come down and get the relevant information from you. Is she at home?"

"Yes."

"I'll be right down."

Sam ran out of her office, startling the rest of the team. "Bob, leave what you're doing and come with me."

"What? Where are we going?"

"Mick Bartlett has been reported missing. We need to visit his wife."

"Holy shit." He snatched his jacket off the back of the chair. "Liam, can you take over from me? I've managed to locate the boss's car but that's as far as I've got."

"Leave it with me, Bob." Liam flew across the room and sat in Bob's seat.

"We shouldn't be long, folks. Ring me if you uncover anything important," Sam shouted and pushed open the door. She ran down the stairs and into reception.

Nick was ready and waiting with all the information she needed. Sam handed the sheet with Bartlett's address to Bob, ready for him to input into the satnav.

"Thanks, Nick. We'll let you know if we need backup. Who knows what we're up against here."

"I'll have a team on full alert for you, ma'am."

Outside, before they got in the car, Bob said, "I'm sensing this isn't good."

Sam cocked an eyebrow, shook her head and slipped behind the steering wheel. "I've heard it all now. Where are we going?"

"Head out towards the Davidsons' farm." He added the necessary details to the satnav, and the machine worked out the route. "Take a left at the end of this road. The next right and right again, and that should be us."

"Remind me when I get closer," Sam replied.

Bob tutted. "You're a detective, you're supposed to be able to retain information."

She jabbed him in the leg with her fist. "I can do without the smartarse remarks, thanks. I wonder what's going on."

"Something sinister by the sounds of it."

"Stating the obvious as usual, partner."

"You asked the question; you should have said if it was rhetorical or not."

His response earned him another jab.

"Once more and I'll put a complaint in for abuse."

Sam laughed. "Yay, two complaints against my name in a week, what joy."

Bob grinned. "As if I would. It's left here."

"I thought you said it was right then two lefts," she replied, deliberately winding him up.

"I give up." He turned the volume up on the satnav and crossed his arms in disgust.

Sam laughed, but Bob refused to join in.

She followed the satnav's instructions and pulled up outside a semi-detached house in a quiet road which consisted of only ten houses. "This is a better area than I thought it was going to be."

"Meaning? Because he's a farmhand he wouldn't be able to afford a decent home?"

Sam swallowed and said, "Yes, shame on me, eh?"

"You said it. Perhaps his wife works as well, so they have two incomes coming in, or they live with their parents, that's not unheard of these days. We won't know until we set foot in the house, but it's not like you to make snap judgements."

"Consider me told. Right, let's stop squabbling and get inside, shall we?"

They approached the front door, and it burst open to reveal a distraught woman in her late thirties standing there, her cheeks tear-stained, and her hands shook when she clasped them to either side of her face.

"Thank God you're here, I've been going out of my mind with worry. I thought you wouldn't take this issue seriously, what with him only going missing this morning. Come in, please, I don't want the neighbours to know our business and to start gossiping about us."

"I'm DI Sam Cobbs, and this is my partner, DS Bob Jones. You must be Tara."

"Yes, that's right. Come through to the lounge. You'll have

to excuse the mess, I decided to tidy up one of the cupboards in there to keep my mind occupied."

"It's no problem."

They followed her into a sizeable lounge with a bay window and a wood-burning stove which was ticking over in the hearth, successfully taking the chill off the room.

"You have a lovely home," Sam said, trying to put the woman at ease from the outset.

"Thank you. My parents left it to us when they passed away a couple of years ago. We're slowly renovating it. This was the first room we tackled, quickly followed by the kitchen, which still had the original nineteen fifties' cabinets in it, not to our taste at all. My parents preferred to spend their money on going abroad two or three times a year and didn't think to bother updating the house."

"Each to their own, eh? You have excellent taste. Why don't we take a seat, and you can tell us what's going on?"

Sam and Bob sat on the sofa, and Tara eased herself into the large armchair on the other side of the coffee table.

"He went off as usual at five this morning. I stayed in bed until seven, then I got the kids up and gave them their breakfast. We all got dressed, and then I walked them to school. Every morning, when I return from the school run, I have a quiet sit down with a coffee and ring Mick. He always answers, without fail. This morning, he didn't." She picked up her phone from the coffee table and scrolled through it. "There, I rang him five times, and it immediately went through to the answerphone. That's not normal, so I knew something must be wrong."

"Wouldn't he be snowed under? Have a bucketload of extra work to do now that Alvin has passed away?"

"Yes, I appreciate that, but it doesn't usually prevent him from answering the phone. He puts it on speaker while he deals with the animals. Today was different. So, sensing something was wrong, I rang the farm. Bethany answered and told me that she was disappointed in Mick. When I asked why, she said that he'd let her down at a time when she needed him the most."

Sam inclined her head. "Did she explain why?"

"She said he hadn't turned up for work. I couldn't believe what I was hearing and told her that he'd set off first thing, the same time as usual. That's when I became scared and kept thinking about what had happened to Alvin. I sat here for an hour or so, arguing with myself. One minute mumbling that everything would be all right, that he'd had a mishap on the way to work, like a burst tyre or something, but then I began to think more logically about that scenario. He would have called me if he was in any type of trouble. Why would his phone go straight to answerphone?" Her hands shook even more as she ran them around her face and through her hair.

"Let's try and remain calm. You're doing great so far. What else did Bethany have to say, anything?"

"Yes, she was a right bitch to me, told me that if he didn't show up for work today, he needn't go back there tomorrow. He's never taken a sick day off work in his life before. She had no right shouting that down the phone to me, especially when I'm at my lowest ebb, out of my mind with worry."

"I agree, she should have been more compassionate and understanding, but on the flip side, her own feelings must be wild and all over the place after losing her husband," Sam said, making excuses for the woman who was at the top of their suspect list.

"I know, but on the other hand, Mick has been at their beck and call for years and never, I repeat *never*, let them down, even when he's received a call at two o'clock in the morning during the lambing season. So, you'll have to forgive me for being irate with the woman."

"I can understand that. I have to ask if your husband has

had any problems with anyone lately."

"Such as? What are you saying here? That you think someone has deliberately taken him because he's had a spat with them?"

"I'm just trying to search for a reason why your husband would go missing when he's usually very reliable about showing up for work and for receiving your calls at a certain time. Can you try ringing him again?"

"Of course." She pushed the dedicated button for her husband's number and put it on speaker so they could all hear. It rang four times before the answerphone kicked in. "Now do you believe me?"

"It's not that I don't believe you, far from it. It's my duty to find out if there might be a plausible reason why your husband may have gone missing this morning. If there's not, then we'll do all we can to assist you and put an alert out for him ASAP."

"Good, do it. Because my husband left here, making a point of telling me what he had planned for the day. He sat there last night, whilst the kids and I watched TV, and made a list of jobs that he intended to do when he got to work today. Now, does that sound to you like someone who was about to take off and not bother showing up for work?"

"No, it doesn't. I'm sorry, it wasn't my intention to upset you."

"Well, you have. If you're not interested in helping me out, then go. I'll borrow a friend's car and search the area between the farm and here myself."

"There's no need for you to do that. Please bear with us, all we're trying to do is ascertain the facts to get an overall picture of what has possibly happened."

"Which I've told you, and you're still sitting here, questioning me when you should be out there looking for him."

"Okay, I'll get a search organised. What route does he

usually take to the farm? And how long does the trip take him to get there?"

"Ten minutes maximum, and there's really only one way he can go. Have you got a map? I don't know the names of the roads, not off the top of my head."

Bob pulled out his mobile and Google Maps appeared on his screen which he angled towards Tara. "The farm is there, and we're here, does he take this road usually?" he asked.

"Yes, that's the one, Fairbanks Lane."

"Can you call it in, Bob?" Sam asked. "Get a couple of patrol cars out that way, see what they can find. Maybe request a dog team to join them."

Bob left the room and made the call from the hallway.

"Can I get you a drink?" Sam asked Tara.

"No, I have had more than my share of coffee this morning. Oh, sorry, was that a hint? Do you want one?"

"Not in the slightest. I'm sorry if we got off on the wrong foot."

"It's okay. I shouldn't have snapped at you. I'm very anxious about Mick."

"Of course you are. Has Mick ever had any issues with Bethany at the farm?"

Tara shook her head and frowned. "Not as far as I know, why?"

"Just ensuring everything was as it should be with their relationship," Sam said, and she mentally kicked herself for wording her question that way.

"Relationship? What are you saying?"

"Employer and employee relationship. Was everything as it should be?"

"I can't possibly comment on that. Mick usually worked alongside Alvin. I might be wrong, but I don't think he had much to do with Bethany, not as such. It was Mick who ran the farm day in and day out. She might have dealt with the paperwork side of things, that's about all. The physical side of running a farm and dealing with the animals was all down to Alvin. Jenny often helped out, perhaps when the weather was good, but never when it was snowing or pouring down with rain."

"Thanks, that gives me a clearer insight into how the farm works," Sam said, despite Bethany giving her the same information a few days earlier. In fact, everyone she'd spoken to so far had a different opinion on the subject.

Bob came back into the room and nodded at Sam. "All done. Two teams are heading out this way now."

"Thanks, Bob. Is there anything else you can think of that might be concerning Mick at this time? Perhaps financial problems, something along those lines?"

"No, nothing that most people in this country aren't having to contend with right now, during this dreadful time. He goes to work and comes home at a reasonable hour most days. Then spends a couple of hours entertaining the kids while I get on with dinner, then I bath the kids and we usually watch a couple of hours of TV. We normally go to bed no later than ten because he starts his day at around five, most days."

"How many days a week does he work at the farm?"

"Six, he has Sundays off, plus the odd Saturday here and there, if the kids have got something special on, like a trip or if my son is playing a football match. Mick is good like that, when they have activities they need to attend at the weekends, makes up for the time he misses out being with them during the week."

"That's a lot of hours Mick puts in every week."

"It is, but he enjoys the job, or he did, when Alvin was alive. They were more like brothers than boss and employee. I know Alvin's death has hit him hard, but we discussed it the night he died, and Mick said he was determined to make a go of the farm and wouldn't see Bethany and Jenny struggle, not on his watch, and now he's gone missing. Why? How could that happen? Is there something else going on that I should know about?"

"We're not sure as yet. Our investigation into Alvin's death is still in its infancy. It's always a struggle trying to find clues during the early stages of a case. But, as a team, we're doing our best."

"But now you have my husband's disappearance to contend with, is that what you're saying?"

"It's an added problem to throw into the mix, one that we'll do our utmost to overcome."

"I hope you find him and quickly. Shouldn't you be out there, looking for him now that I've given you all the details regarding his disappearance?"

"Yes, we're going to stop by the farm first, and there are a couple of patrol cars doing their bit to find your husband. Actually, you can do one last thing for me."

"What's that?"

"Tell us what car he drives and give us the registration number, if you know it."

"Now you're asking. No idea on the reg, sorry, but it's a red Ford Fiesta. I think it's a 2017 model, if that helps?"

"It does, we can check the other details. Is it registered to this address?"

"That's correct."

Sam and Bob both stood, and Tara showed them to the front door.

"Please, please find him. He's all I've got now my parents are no longer with us. I have the children, of course, but that's different."

"We're going to do all we can to bring him home to you, I promise."

"Thank you."

CHAPTER 6

When they showed up at the farm, Sam and Bob exited the car. Bethany Davidson was on her way to the barn with a bucket of feed, and she seemed surprised to see them.

"Let's see what the Weeping Widow has to say," Sam said.

"Harsh."

"Is it? We'll soon see if I'm wrong about her. We just need that one clue to fall into our laps to get this investigation on the right track."

They got out of the car and walked towards the barn. Bethany hadn't hung around to wait for them. She'd entered the barn, and they found her feeding the pigs.

"Hello, Bethany. How are you?"

"I was fine until this morning, when Mick failed to show up for work. Luckily, I had set my alarm and was able to fill in and do his chores for him."

"It's very unfortunate. We've just come from speaking with Tara."

"How is she?"

"Distraught, as you can imagine. So, are you telling me that Mick never showed up here at all this morning?"

"That's right. I told Tara that when she rang earlier. Why, are you disputing it?"

"I'm not, I was simply clarifying the details. We've tried ringing his phone several times, but it's diverting to the answerphone."

"And what do you expect me to do about it?" Bethany said, her lip curled.

"I was merely stating facts. Did he mention yesterday that he was going to stop off for supplies or something on the way to work?"

"No, that's not his responsibility, that will be down to me going forward. I'll be organising the daily running of this place now that my husband is no longer with us. I would never let a mere farmhand take on the task of doing that."

"But you're going to need some help, running the farm and all it entails, aren't you?"

Bethany frowned. "Obviously. That's why I employ Mick, but if he chooses not to show up for work then there's very little I can do about it. Maybe he and Tara fell out this morning and she's covering her tracks and not telling you the truth."

"Do they argue a lot?"

"I don't know. I haven't got a sticky beak, I keep my nose out of peoples' domestic business, especially if it doesn't affect the farm. Only this time it has."

"Well, we have a couple of patrols out there searching for Mick's car because, according to what Tara has just told us, everything was as it should have been at home when he set off this morning."

"And? So you thought you'd come here and hassle me? Is this payback for me putting in a complaint about the way you treated me on your last visit?"

It was Sam's turn to frown. "Not in the slightest. It's your prerogative to complain about me if you believe I treated you appallingly. That is what you said, wasn't it?"

"I might have, because that's how I remember it. I caught you talking to Mick behind my back."

"I wasn't talking about you as such, as I explained at the time. Anyway, that's in the past. We're still dealing with your husband's death. Some information has come to light that we're looking into but, as Mick worked alongside your husband daily, it's our duty to come here and see where the land lies, if you will."

Bethany's eyes narrowed, and she took a step towards Sam. "What new information are you talking about? I have a right to know."

"Ah, maybe I shouldn't have said anything just yet, that was remiss of me, until we have delved further into the incident in question."

The woman's eyes narrowed further, forming tiny slits, and she dropped the bucket. "This is bullshit. You're trying to get a reaction out of me. I'm warning you, if you're intent on messing with me, there's only going to be one outcome."

Sam tilted her head. "Sorry, is that some kind of threat, Mrs Davidson?"

Bethany smiled and shook her head. "No, not really. More a piece of wise advice. Now, if you'll excuse me, I have over five hundred animals that need feeding before lunchtime and I'm only halfway through the task because I'm two men down now, not just one."

"We won't hold you up any longer than is necessary. Is there anyone you can call to give you a hand?"

"In a word, no."

"Okay, what about Jenny, is she around? Can she not help you out for a few days?"

"No, she's still too distraught and refuses to get out of her pit in the morning. She'll surface mid-afternoon, as usual, expecting me to care for her every whim, no doubt. As if I have time to cook homemade nutritional meals nowadays, when I have all of this to attend to."

"I'm sorry to hear that. Grief takes its toll on people in different ways. I'm sure a little understanding wouldn't go amiss. I'm not making excuses for her, but she's young and has lost both of her parents now. That can be a lot to handle for someone her age."

"Are you insinuating that the grief isn't affecting me? I assure you, it bloody is. But I have to push that aside, otherwise, if I were to sit in the house wallowing in self-pity, the animals would suffer, and that would bring the authorities banging on my door. You'd like that, wouldn't you?"

"No, not at all. I appreciate that life goes on for you all. Maybe Jenny is feeling her father's death more because of her age."

"Ah, right, so we've got to make exceptions for the young, is that it? Don't you think I have enough on my plate, with Mick failing to show up for work? Life's shit at times, it's something everyone in this universe has to battle with on a daily basis. We can't come grinding to a halt if we have responsibilities. We're self-employed and, at times such as this, it's one more hurdle we have to tackle."

"I get that. What about the farming community? Can you not reach out to them for help? Is there a governing body that you can turn to in emergencies?"

"Ha, I'm not one for having strangers on the premises, nosing into my business. I'd rather cope with things on my own, even more so now that Mick has gone AWOL."

"Maybe you have to be willing to be open to getting help from others. If not, I fear the pressure might begin to take its toll on you mentally as well as financially."

"Surely that's my business and is nothing to do with you."

Sam shrugged. "Sorry, just offering an opinion, for what it's worth."

"If I want expert farming advice, I won't come knocking on your door anytime soon, but thanks for caring."

Sam smiled. "On that note, I think we'll leave you to it. If anything comes to light regarding Mick's disappearance or if he should show up for work during the day, will you give me a call to let me know?"

"I'll be sure to do that. Now, if you'll excuse me, I have work to do, even if you haven't."

With that, she rushed out of the door. Sam faced her partner and stared at him.

Bob shrugged. "I guess that told us."

Sam marched out of the barn seconds later. By that time, Bethany was nowhere to be seen. They returned to the car. Sam refused to react, except internally, just in case the woman was hiding, watching them. Instead, she started the engine and drew away from the farm. She had a dilemma on her hands. Did she go back to the station or stay in the vicinity, searching for Mick?

"I can see the cogs turning. What are you thinking?" Bob asked after a few moments' silence had filled the car once they got on the road.

"I know we want to get on with Alvin's investigation, but I'm in two minds as to whether we should stay out here, join in the search. Something in my gut is telling me to remain in the area. What do you think? Am I talking bullshit?"

"You? Talk bullshit? Never!"

His sarcasm earnt him a thump in the thigh that he wasn't expecting. He yelped, and she grinned at him.

"Now, do you want to answer the question properly?"

"As always, you need to listen to your gut. It has served you well in the past, hasn't it?"

"True. Right, get the map up. We'll take a look at the area, see if we can pinpoint any areas where he might have likely been abducted."

Sam left the main road and drew into a narrow farm track. Bob brought up the map on his phone and studied the area surrounding them.

"Are there any farm buildings which might be derelict, or farmhouses, come to that?"

"Not that I can see. How far do you want me to search?"

"A couple of miles' radius. It depends on the road, doesn't it? Our backs are against the wall if there is only one main route he could have taken to the Davidsons' place."

"What if someone flagged him down, he pulled over to lend them a hand and received a whack over the head, then the perp stole the car and dumped him miles away?"

She sighed. "It's going to be an impossible task, isn't it?"

"You could say that. The truth is, what's happened to him is pure speculation until any evidence to the contrary comes our way. How many times during a past investigation have we wasted time out in the field, searching for a missing person, instead of getting on with the real work back at base?"

Sam started the engine. "You're right. I'm clearly not thinking straight about this. Let's get back to the station."

They hadn't driven more than half a mile when Sam's mobile rang.

"Hello, DI Sam Cobbs. How can I help?"

"Sorry to trouble you, ma'am. I'm Constable Wainwright, I've been assigned to search the area for a Mick Bartlett."

"Ah, yes. How's it going?"

"We believe we've located his car."

"Where? Can you give me your coordinates?"

"We're down by the River Derwent on Fairbanks Lane."

"How far down the road? Anything else in the area that can give us an indication of your exact location?"

"Not really. We're about a mile down the road. The satnav is playing up, not giving me a definite location."

"Okay, we're not far from you. Hang tight." Sam ended the call and eased her foot down on the accelerator.

"The constable didn't mention Bartlett, only that he had found the car."

"I know, that's the worrying part. Still, we need to remain positive about this. At least it's one step further than we were five minutes ago."

They travelled one more mile, and then Bob pointed ahead of them.

"There they are, unless that's stating the obvious. I know your eyesight isn't the best these days."

"Cheeky git." Sam put her foot down and before long they arrived at the scene.

She and Bob leapt out of the car to speak with the constable and his partner.

"No one in the vicinity? Just the car?" she enquired.

"It's as we found it, ma'am. The driver's door was open when we got here, no one in the area, and no other vehicles nearby, either."

Sam took a few steps to the right of her to check the riverbank immediately beyond the car. As far as she could tell there were no fresh footprints in the muddy bank that led down to the fast-flowing river. "Is it too much to assume he's ended up in there? Is that what someone wants us to believe?" She walked back to the vehicle, inserted her fingers into a pair of nitrile gloves and inspected the interior of the car. Tucked into the centre console was a wallet. She removed it and flipped it open to examine the contents. There were several cards including a debit and credit card, both in the name of Mr M Bartlett.

"Is it his?" Bob asked.

"Yep. I think we can rule a robbery out." Upon further

inspection, she found two twenties and a tenner in the pouch at the back. She removed the notes and waved them at Bob.

"Shit!" he said.

Sam stared off into the distance, contemplating the circumstances as to why Mick had likely pulled over. Not for the first time, several different scenarios ran through her mind, none of them positive ones. They had already learnt that there were no other houses or buildings on this stretch of the road, as they were in the middle of nowhere. She moved to the rear of the car and lashed out at the top of it. "Shit, he's been rear-ended, probably forced off the road."

"Similar to what happened to you," Bob said. "We need to get SOCO out here, see if they can pick up any fragments of paint on the bumper and match it to the car that shunted you."

"You read my mind. Make the call, Bob."

Sam mulled over the incident he'd referred to that had taken place the previous evening, and the danger she had found herself in. She shook her head over and over. Could it possibly be the same person who'd attacked her? What was their intention? To force her off the road and abduct her? A shudder rippled up her spine. If she hadn't had the foresight to switch on the blues and twos during the incident, where the hell would she be right now? And more to the point, what the heck has happened to Mick?

"They're on their way," Bob muttered, interrupting her train of thoughts. "Are you all right?"

"I'm not sure. I think so. I've got that many scenarios and questions rattling around in my head right now."

"I'm not surprised. I'm surmising all to do with the incident that you were entangled in, am I right?"

"One hundred percent. What the hell is going on here? What if there's a link? It seems probable more than possible at this stage. Why would someone try and take me out?"

"I might be stating the obvious here, probably because you're the lead detective on the investigation."

"But why? Or is that a dumb question? It was rhetorical by the way. I've been the lead investigator on hundreds of investigations throughout my career and I've never been in this situation before, so why this time?"

"Criminals getting bolder. You getting closer to nailing the perpetrator? Someone intent on scaring you, warning you to back off?"

Sam raised an eyebrow. "Well, that's not likely to happen, is it? Why would I back off?"

Bob hitched up his shoulders. "I'm just putting it out there. Not everyone has the privilege of working with you. Or recognises dogged determination when they see it."

Sam smiled, the first time she'd felt like doing that in a few hours. "I guess, that's one thing in our favour. Let's do a brief search of the area, guys, not too close to the vehicle. I'd hate to miss anything obvious while we're waiting for SOCO to turn up."

They all took a few steps back and scoured the area for the next ten minutes but came up blank. Sam returned to the riverbank, and Bob joined her.

"Do you think we should organise a dive team?"

Bob groaned and heaved out a breath. "I think we'd be foolish not to. If word got out that one hadn't been organised, you could take some flack from the media."

"Yeah, you're right. Okay, I'll do that now." Sam called the station and spoke to Nick, asked him to organise the dive team, then she requested that a K9 team also joined them at the scene.

Nick asked her to hold the line and then moments later told her a team should be with them within twenty minutes.

Sam decided to wait in the car with Bob until the reinforcements arrived. "I hate hanging around, waiting for people."

"What else can we do?" Bob asked.

Sam removed her mobile from her pocket and rang the station again. This time she spoke with Claire and apprised her of the situation, informing her that they would be held up for a while. "Any news at your end, Claire?"

"Frustratingly, not much, boss. The system keeps crashing. I've been on the phone to IT, and they've told me the matter is in hand and that we've all got to be patient."

"Jesus Christ, they need to live in the real world. What are we supposed to do in the meantime, sit around on our hands all day long?"

"I said pretty much the same thing to the bloke myself. I'm sure they have no idea what our job entails on a daily basis."

"Okay, as frustrating as it is, stick with it. Can I have a brief chat with Liam?"

"Sure. Liam, the boss wants a word with you," Claire called across the room.

Liam came on the line a few seconds later. "Yes, boss?"

"Anything on the footage yet?"

"Still trying to find the car, boss. Cameras are few and far between in that part of the town."

"I knew it was a long shot. The thing is, we've found Mick's car—not him, just his car—and by the looks of it, it has been rear-ended. Ring a bell, does it?"

"Bugger. Okay, I'll widen the search, see what I can find in relation to the incident you were involved in. Are you asking me to deal with two searches now?"

"If you haven't got the time, how about passing this one over to Oliver?"

"Good idea. There's not a lot else we can do, not with us struggling to keep the system online at present. I'll have a word. Can you give me the location where the vehicle was found?"

"I can, roughly. Hang on, maybe you can check the coordinates of where I am by using the tracker on my phone."

"I'll do that. What car am I searching for?"

"Mick Bartlett's is a red Ford Fiesta. Do your best for me."

"Don't I always, boss?"

"You do. Speak later."

She ended the call and again studied the area around them, in every direction. "Was it intentional? To attack Mick out here?"

"Probably. What if the perpetrator tried to force him off the road and into the river? I spotted a slight skid mark back there."

"I noticed it, too. Where is he, Bob? Is he dead or alive? What does this have to do with Alvin's death? They're obviously connected."

"Do you still suspect Bethany?"

"Hard not to, given her attitude towards us, or should I say, me, at the farm today."

"I can't make her out. It's a hard one to call in the circumstances, after her losing her husband and the amount of work she has on her plate. In her defence, maybe it was the stress talking earlier."

"Possibly. You're a better person than me, Bob, at least you're prepared to give her the benefit of the doubt. Frankly, there are too many coincidences, for my liking, for me not to be suspicious of the woman. Her mood swings are only adding to the melting pot."

"Fair enough. Again, it comes down to proof and any evidence that comes our way in the meantime."

"Absolutely. Which is why I haven't jumped the gun yet and hauled her arse into the station for questioning. I have her complaint hanging over my head for one thing, that is making me more cautious than I'd usually be. I just hope that doesn't prove to be detrimental to the case, come the end."

"I've told you already, you need to stick with your gut instinct but, on the other hand, maybe taking a step back will be the way to go for now."

Sam chewed over his suggestion for a while, even though it didn't sit comfortably with her. She glanced in her rear-view mirror. "SOCO are here, finally. I wonder how long the K9 and the dive team are going to take to get here."

"Patience was a virgin and all that," Bob quipped. "It hasn't been that long since we placed the calls."

"I know. I'm anxious to get on with things." She jumped out of the car and approached the van.

"Ah, Inspector, we meet again."

Sam smiled at the technician who had helped her out first thing, taking a sample from her bumper. "Ah, we do indeed. Similar scenario on this one. It would appear the driver took a shunt from behind. I'm not one who is inclined to believe in coincidences, I'd rather use science to help me ascertain the facts. If you can match the paint to the same car that hit mine, it'll be plain sailing for us when we finally track down the person responsible."

"Rightio, let's do our best and see what we can do for you then."

"Cheers, I appreciate it."

"Do you know what happened? Was the driver injured in the incident?" the tech asked.

"The honest answer is, I don't know. The driver was reported missing earlier, we've only just discovered his vehicle. He was nowhere to be seen. There's a slight skid mark on the road back there. We're presuming another car rear-ended him, possibly tried to force him into the river. Maybe he realised what was about to happen and jumped out of the vehicle."

"And then disappeared into thin air, I take it?"

"That appears to be how the story ends, yes. I found the victim's wallet still in the car. If it was an intended robbery, the perpetrator failed to locate his cards and money. I find that incredibly hard to believe."

"I'm inclined to agree with you. Okay, leave this with me, I'll see what I can do for you."

Another vehicle approached. It was a patrol car. The dog barked in the back as she got closer, putting her on edge. She'd had a chunk taken out of her arm by a German Shepherd when she was a teenager and had been a tad wary of them ever since. The officers got out, and they introduced themselves.

"Constable Adams, ma'am. Here to assist you any which way we can."

"Great to hear. We're desperate to find any kind of lead you can detect for us." She gave him a rundown of what she perceived had happened to Mick Bartlett.

Adams' gaze shifted up and down the road and ended up on the river behind them. "Is there a chance he might have ended up in the river?"

"You tell me. That's why we've called you out to assist us."

"We'll see what we can find. Do you have anything belonging to the victim that Troy can use for scent?"

"I have his wallet, if that's any good?"

"It'll do if you haven't found anything else."

Sam handed him a pair of gloves to put on and then the wallet. "If you have a problem, I could ask one of the techs to see what's in the boot."

He cocked an eyebrow and asked, "Hasn't anyone thought to do that yet?"

Sam winced. She'd been so intent on preserving the scene that she'd forgotten rule two million and twenty-three in the police handbook: instructing officers to search all parts of an abandoned vehicle, including the boot. "Damn, I'll get SOCO to do it now."

"I'll keep Troy out of the way until you issue further instructions."

"Thanks." Sam went back to the techs standing at the rear of their van and sheepishly asked, "Any chance you can check the boot for me?"

"You haven't done it?"

"I was conscious about preserving the scene. Sorry."

"No problem. Give us two minutes to get our gear together."

Sam smiled and walked back to the car to join Bob.

"What's going on?" he asked.

"We have to wait for them to get their equipment out. I've also asked them to open the boot."

"Shit. We should have checked that, shouldn't we?"

"Yep, I think we both screwed up there."

"Let's hope not, or maybe that's the wrong thing to say, if they find his body in there."

"We'll soon find out." Sam spent the next five minutes pacing until the SOCO techs finally got down to business and approached the car. The boot opened in slow motion, at least it seemed that way to Sam. She inched forward, her gaze never leaving the tech, trying to gauge his reaction. There wasn't one. What did that mean? That he was a good poker player or that there was nothing obvious lying in the boot?

The temptation proved too much for Sam, and she closed the distance between her and the tech team. "Well?"

"You might want to come and have a look for yourself, Inspector."

Sam closed her eyes for the briefest of moments and exhaled the stale breath burning her lungs. "Shit."

The tech stood to one side and issued a warning, "Don't get too close, not without the appropriate attire on."

"I won't. Crap," she said, once the boot came into full view.

Bob snuck up behind her and let out half a dozen worse expletives.

"Exactly." Sam returned to Constable Adams and shook her head. "I guess we won't be needing your services after all. Sorry to have wasted your time."

"That's a shame. Glad you've discovered his body, though, that'll be a huge relief to his family."

"No doubt. Thanks again."

Sam returned to the vehicle. "Have either of you contacted the pathologist?"

"Yes, I took the liberty of calling him. He'll be here within twenty minutes."

AFTER DES SHOWED up and confirmed the victim's death was from a gunshot wound, Sam left the scene and drove to Tara's house to break the news. As expected, the poor woman collapsed into a heap, a distraught and utter mess. Sam had to call her sister, Monica, and ask her to sit with Tara while Sam and Bob got on with the investigation.

Back at the station, the team were all subdued. Everyone had played their part in trying to find Mick, but it proved to be too little too late because he'd been dead all along.

"Why didn't we check the damn car as soon as we found it?" Sam complained in her office as they began to unwind after their traumatic day.

"Stop with the recriminations. We weren't to know. Anyway, I'm as guilty as you in that respect. Look at it this way, if there's a bullet or some shot left in his body, that's going to be the first real piece of evidence to come our way."

"Hmm... you might have something there. Most farmers have guns, don't they?"

"You're thinking Bethany again."

"Aren't you?" She paused for a second or two and shook her head.

"What's going on in that mind of yours now?" Bob asked.

"He was rear-ended. What if I hadn't had the foresight to bring attention to myself last night?" She shuddered at the thought.

"You can't go through life saying, 'what if?', you know that, Sam. It didn't happen. It's best not to dwell on how things might have turned out."

"I know. No matter what words of wisdom you're trying to offer me, it's still not going to stop me from going over the scene in my head and considering what the outcome might have been if my car hadn't been fitted with the lights and a siren."

"It wouldn't have come to that. Someone set out to scare you, that's all."

"But how do you know that? You don't, end of."

"Yes, end of... the day. Why don't we wrap things up and start over again in the morning?"

"Okay, you win. I'm mentally and physically exhausted this evening."

CHAPTER 7

It turned out to be a busy couple of days for the team. But Sam sensed there was more angst to come when she set foot into the station the following Monday morning. She'd had a relaxing weekend with her family on the Sunday and, as promised, Doreen had joined them, her ankle nearly back to normal with the aid of the support that Sam had lent her. When Sam had laid eyes on her father, she'd been shocked by how much weight he'd lost since her mother had passed away and she'd said as much to her sister.

"We're doing our best for him, taking him extra meals when we can, but you know how it is. At the end of a long day, you don't always want to cook a decent meal and have to rely on the takeaway to see you through. Dad's not overly keen on them so needs to fend for himself now and again."

And he clearly wasn't doing very well in that department. As a family unit, they'd agreed they would all chip in where possible and meet up regularly once a week for a family meal. Sam had insisted such an event should take place at the weekend, knowing how long her shifts could be during the week with a double murder to solve.

"Monday morning, a new week dawns, I wonder what excitement it will bring with it," Sam announced before the team's usual meeting got underway.

"Let's hope the body count doesn't rise this week, we've got enough on our plates as it is," Bob replied.

"Only time will tell. Which reminds me, I need to get on to the pathologist first thing. I still haven't received the PM report for Mick Bartlett, yet. Actually, I'll do it now. Keep going through where we ended up last week, folks." Sam entered her office, ignored the post filling her in-tray and sat behind her desk to make the call. "Ah, I've caught you, Mr Markham."

"You have. Who is this?"

"I'm offended you don't recognise my voice by now. It's Sam."

"I have news for you, I did, I was messing with you. What can I do for you on this frosty January morning, Inspector?"

"I was wondering if you had the PM report ready for me yet."

"You're in luck. I was at my desk at seven this morning, typing up two reports, one of them for Mr Bartlett. As soon as I've cast an eye over it for any possible typos, it'll be winging its way to you. So, check your inbox in twenty minutes or so."

"Anything important in it?"

"What are you insinuating? That my other PM reports are boring and lack content?"

"No, that's not what I was saying at all, and you know it."

He laughed. "Lighten up. When are you going to realise I enjoy pulling your leg now and again?"

"Pass. I can never tell with you because you can be off-hand most of the time."

He gasped. "Well, now you've offended me. I wouldn't necessarily call it that."

"Oh, pray tell, what would you call it then?"

"Being professional and going about my work in an efficient manner, how's that?"

Sam coughed into her hand and whispered, "Bullshit."

"How dare you! Anyway, I haven't got time to spend chatting on the phone all day. Is there anything else you need from me?"

"No, just that report. Oh, yes, wait. What about the shot used? Have forensics come back with anything from that yet? Or is it still too early?"

"Let me check the system, see what I can find."

Sam flicked through the envelopes in her tray while she waited.

"Ah, yes, here it is. It came through over the weekend. I must have missed it, otherwise I would have added it to my report."

"And what does it say?"

"It's a smaller pellet, birdshot."

"Hmm... the type a farmer might use?"

"Yes, highly plausible."

"Okay, yet another nail in her coffin," Sam mumbled, more to herself than to Des.

But she'd forgotten how keen his hearing was.

"What are you saying? That you have a suspect in mind?"

"I've had her in mind since day one, I just needed the proof to back up my suspicions, and now you've given it to me."

"Are you going to share the details or keep me guessing?"

"The first victim's wife, Bethany Davidson."

"Ah, okay. What about the car? Don't forget that aspect."

"I won't. I need to get everything in order first. She's the type who, given the chance, will go out of her way to run rings around us."

"I know the type. Well, I must fly, you know where I am if you need me. Dare I say it, I think you have enough to fling at her now."

"I'm getting there. Thanks, Des."

"I'll send the report through soon. Stand by for it."

"I will. In the meantime, I'll deal with my least favourite chore of the day, my post."

"Have fun. Speak soon."

"No doubt."

Sam ended the call and narrowed her eyes as she gazed out of the window. *It all appears to be coming together now; however, I still need to bide my time. The last thing I want to do is blow it. I need to nail her with every piece of evidence going. I've been caught out before, jumping in too early. I swore it would never happen again. So, crossing the T's and dotting the I's is a must if we're going to get her bang to rights.*

What with one thing or another, Sam had forgotten to inform Bethany after they had discovered Mick's body. This had led to Sam receiving an irate phone call the next day from Bethany for 'keeping her out of the loop'. It went against the grain for Sam to apologise to the woman, nevertheless, that's exactly what she did. Rather than feel the wrath of the DCI at the prospect of having another complaint made against her. Sam had tried to reason with Bethany, told her that by the time she had shared the news with Tara Bartlett and got the second investigation underway, ringing Bethany, as promised, had completely gone out of her mind. But Bethany was having none of it and had shouted at Sam, insisted she should be more professional, which had stung, but Sam had shrugged off the insult moments later after she'd hung up.

When she'd informed her partner of the call, he'd wagged

his finger and warned, "You're playing a dangerous game with that one, Sam. I wouldn't be in a rush to mess with her head, if I were you."

Sam had grinned at him and pointed at her chest. "Me? Would I do that?"

Sam rejoined her team after briefly going over the post and glancing through the PM report once that had arrived. "Right, on the agenda this morning is for Bob and I to visit Jenny Davidson at work. She was due back today, if I recall?"

"That's right. I'll look up the address for the salon," Bob replied.

Sam went back into the office to collect her jacket. By the time she returned, Bob had the information to hand and was waiting for her at the door.

THE SALON WAS LARGER than expected and situated on the edge of the shopping precinct in Workington. A receptionist with spiky green hair smiled and welcomed them.

Sam produced her ID. "DI Sam Cobbs and DS Bob Jones to see Jenny Davidson, if she's free."

"Ah, there's a problem with that."

Sam inclined her head. "What type of problem? Is she here or not?"

"Wait just a second, I'll get Andrea to come and speak to you."

Before Sam could question her further, the young girl slipped through a door off to her left and returned with a woman in her early forties with long blonde hair.

"Can I help? I'm the manager of this establishment."

Sam introduced herself once more and asked, "Is it possible to speak with Jenny?"

"It might be, if she had shown up for work this morning. I've had it with that girl letting me down. And before you have a go at me, yes, I'm aware that she's recently lost her father, but it's called life—it goes on, for most people. I've got a business to run. She rang me on Friday, assured me that she would be coming back today, and she's let me down. I made sure her diary was full, you know, to help keep her mind off things, and this is how she repays me. No phone call, nothing. I'm sorry, but there's no way back for her, not when she's let me down this badly."

"Have you tried calling her?"

"No, why should I? It's her responsibility to ring me, not the other way around. When you see her, tell her not to bother coming back here. I'll get someone reliable to fill her shoes."

"Can't you hold her position open for a few days? Perhaps there's a reasonable explanation as to why she hasn't shown up today."

"No. I need to set an example with the staff. If I let one stylist get away with murder, then they'll all jump on the bandwagon. How will I be able to run a business like that? The answer is I won't, it'll be impossible. People need to appreciate they have a job worth having these days. Most don't. It's her loss, not mine."

"I'm sorry you feel that way. We'll try and find out what has happened and get back to you, if that's all right?"

Andrea shook her head and raised a hand. "Nope, it's not going to happen. If someone clearly doesn't respect me enough to keep me informed about their personal life, then I have no room for them in my salon. We're working through difficult times at present, and people need to appreciate how easy their lives are."

"Easy? As in her work here? Bearing in mind she's just lost her father, so a little empathy wouldn't go amiss."

"I've shown it, numerous times over the past year or so,

and to have that thrown back in my face is… well, galling to say the least."

Sam frowned. "Care to enlighten us as to what you mean by that sweeping statement?"

"She's let me down on a number of occasions. Family issues at the farm that she has no right allowing to disrupt the way this salon works. Like I said before, I need to have reliable staff I can count on, not ones who see this place as a joke sometimes."

"Family issues? Can you tell us more about that?"

Andrea glanced at her watch. "I have a client due in ten minutes, I can spare you five at the most."

"That'd be great. In your office perhaps?"

"Sasha, give me a buzz the second Mrs Fischer arrives."

"I will, boss."

"Come this way." Andrea led them up a short corridor to a bright office at the rear that was decorated with ice-white walls and had pink accessories dotted around the room. There was even a pink feather boa wrapped around a fluorescent sign bearing the owner's name.

Andrea sat up straight behind her glass desk and intertwined her fingers in front of her.

"Perhaps you can tell us a bit more regarding Jenny's family issues?"

"Where do I start? She was always tired when she came to work. Told me that she had to work long hours on the farm after she got home from here at night. Also, her weekends were taken up feeding the animals they have up there. Whether she was just saying that, who bloody knows these days?"

"During the summer, not in the winter, right?"

"No, all year round. That woman, her stepmother, can't remember her damn name now, she told Jenny that if she didn't buck up her ideas, she was going to kick her out."

Bob removed his notebook from his pocket and jotted down the information.

"I see. We were under the impression that Jenny worked a few hours on the farm during the summer but not in the winter."

"Who told you that?"

"Bethany, her stepmother."

"That woman... evil stepmother might be more appropriate."

"Do you know her? Or are you going by hearsay from Jenny?"

"A bit of both. That woman came in here one lunchtime and started an argument with Jenny while she was dealing with a customer. I had nipped out to the baker's and was livid when I returned and saw them at it. I told her to leave straight away. Jenny was so upset, I had to forgo my lunch and take over dying her client's hair. Not ideal, as you can imagine. I felt sorry for the poor girl, told her to take the rest of the day off, but she insisted carrying on with her shift. I got the impression that she didn't know where else to go and didn't want to go back to the farm. Who could blame her after that bitch verbally tearing her to shreds?"

"That's sad. Can you tell us when this happened?"

"Gosh, now you're asking, about three to four months ago."

"And do you know what the argument was about?"

"Jenny going to college, or signing up for a course. Bethany said she was being selfish and should help around the farm more. Jenny said she did enough and was desperate to do something for herself. Bethany told her if she felt that way she should branch out on her own, get a flat by herself. Jenny burst into tears and said she couldn't afford it because of how much Bethany took off her in rent."

"Did Jenny tell you how much that was?"

Andrea lowered her gaze to her hands. "I sat her down for a few minutes at the end of her shift and asked her that very question. She told me that Bethany bullied her into handing over ninety percent of her wages every week."

"Jesus, leaving her with ten percent to cover the necessities in life."

"Precisely. It's unthinkable, isn't it?"

Sam got the impression that Andrea was now regretting kicking off in the reception area. "If she's struggling, won't you reconsider giving her the sack? It seems to me she's desperate to get away from the farm. If you take her job away from her, can you imagine how she's going to cope, being there, on call every day? Especially now her father has gone." She resisted the temptation to tell her about Mick and the part he had once played in running the farm.

"Okay. Maybe I spouted my mouth off out there and regret my actions now. I'm willing to help her in any way I can, but she's got to request it."

"We'll let her know. Thanks for speaking with us today."

They all stood, and Andrea showed them back to the reception area.

"We really appreciate you chatting with us. Thanks for all your help, Andrea."

"You're welcome. I'm not usually an uncaring boss, the other girls will tell you that."

"I'm sure. Let's call it a heat-of-the-moment kind of incident, how about that?"

"Yes, let's do that. Tell Jenny to ring me when she gets a chance, if you get to see her."

"I'll do that. Take care."

They left the salon and made their way back to the car.

"That was an eye-opener," Bob said.

"Wasn't it? I suggest we head back out to the farm and have a chat with Jenny, make sure she's okay."

"If you can get past the evil stepmother. Strange that she hasn't shown up for work or even rung her boss."

"Yeah, that's what is causing doubts in my mind, too. I hope she's all right. We haven't spoken to her or laid eyes on her in over a week now."

"God, don't say that. We've been so consumed with investigating the two murders that we've been guilty of pushing her aside, shall we say?"

"I'd rather not, even if it is the truth." Sam switched on her siren and turned it off again once she got close to the farm.

"You're going to need to keep calm. There's obviously an underlying thing going on between the two of you."

Sam laughed. "Is that you offering me advice on how to conduct myself with a suspect?"

"Is she?"

"Aren't you putting her in that category?"

"I'm still not sure, and yes, I might have a few splinters in my arse to prove I've been sitting on the fence for a while."

"Well, I'm not up for volunteering to pull them out. I bet I prove you wrong before the weekend arrives."

"I hope you do. This case has been a pain in the arse, pun intended, from day one. Can't stand any form of confrontation, you know that."

Sam chuckled. "If that's how you feel, maybe you should consider changing careers."

"Why? That would mean I give up working alongside you all day. I'd never cope without your sparkling character keeping me cheerful through these long, dark days."

Sam's nose wrinkled. "Whatever. I can see why Abigail keeps you busy with DIY projects at night if she has to listen to that kind of drivel in the evenings."

"Damn cheek. I'll have you know we spend hours talking when we go to bed at night, unlike most couples I know."

"Too much information again. We're almost there now. Back into professional mode, it's always good to prepare ourselves for what lies ahead."

"Yeah, at least we know what we're getting with Bethany Davidson."

Sam laughed again. "There is that." She drove through the open gate of the farmyard and drew up outside the house. "Are you ready for this?"

"Yep, the question is, are you?"

"As I'll ever be. Let's see if she allows us to speak with Jenny. My guess is she won't."

"Forever the pessimist."

As they got out of the car, the front door opened and Bethany appeared. She crossed her arms instantly, giving Sam the impression that she was ready to go into battle with them.

"Hello, Mrs Davidson. How are you?"

"I was doing okay until you showed up. What the dickens do you want now? To hassle me some more, or have you come to tell me that you've caught my husband's killer?"

"No, sorry to disappoint you. It's not you who we've come to see, it's Jenny. Is she around?"

"She isn't."

"Oh, may I ask where she is?"

"At her brother's in Penrith, the last I heard."

"I see. Can you give me his address and phone number?"

"Why?"

"Because I need to have a chat with Jenny, that's why."

Bethany huffed out a breath and left them standing on the doorstep. Sam rolled her eyes at Bob who smiled and mouthed, "Be patient."

Sam pulled a face at him. She knew he was talking sense but, inside, her stomach was tied up in knots and her blood was ripping through her veins like molten lava. The more she had to deal with this woman the more she was rankled by her.

As expected, Bethany took a while to come to the door again, and when she did, there was no sign of an apology for keeping them waiting.

"Here you go." She shoved a piece of paper at Sam and closed the door on them.

Sam and Bob walked back to the car. She noticed that the pigs were squealing in the barn and decided to investigate what was going on.

"Where are you going?" Bob shouted from the other side of the car.

"The pigs sound like they're in trouble. Stay there, I won't be long." She folded the piece of paper and put it in her jacket pocket. Sam pushed open the barn door and had to cup her hands over her ears. The noise was deafening, much worse inside than out.

How could that woman allow this to happen? The pigs need feeding. She can't just ignore them. They have basic rights.

She spotted one of the mother pigs lying on the bed of straw that was soiled. The piglets were ramming her stomach, trying to get milk out of her. Sam took a few steps closer to the sow, and unexpected tears pricked her eyes when she realised the pig was dead.

"What the fuck are you doing in here?" Bethany shouted from behind her.

Sam spun around to face the irate woman. "Why are you neglecting them? This sow is dead, and it seems to be distressing the others. Listen to them. Are you telling me you couldn't hear this racket from the house?"

"Get out of here. You have no right being in here. This is none of your business. You think you're a bloody expert with the workings of a farm, you know nothing. The sow is sleeping."

"That's bullshit. Call a vet immediately. We're not leaving here until you do."

"Is that a threat?"

"Yes. *Call the damn vet*. I want to see what an expert has to say about the situation."

"And who is going to pay the bill? You? Because I can't afford it."

"If I have to, yes. I refuse to stand by and let innocent animals suffer because you can't be bothered to feed them."

"Seriously? You have no idea what you're talking about," Bethany said through gritted teeth.

"Give them some food. Now."

Bethany marched towards her and encroached on her personal space. Sam could feel the woman's hot breath on her face.

"Don't give me orders on my own farm, you hear me? You know nothing. Now get out of here or I'll be forced to put another complaint in about your conduct. Ensure your senior officer knows that you're intent on harassing me."

"Do what you want. I'll feed the pigs myself. Tell me where their food is, or I'll rip this place apart to find it."

Bethany's chest rose and fell rapidly, and her eyes formed tiny slits. "You've got five seconds to remove yourself from this barn. Five, four, three, two…"

"Or what?" Bob shouted from the doorway. "Back away from the inspector, Mrs Davidson."

Bethany finally relented and retreated a couple of steps. Then the tears began to fall. "You're putting pressure on me. All this is your fault, keep coming here, badgering me." She dropped to her knees and buried her head in her hands.

Bob leapt into action and tore into the barn. He got down on his haunches beside her and wrapped a reassuring arm around her shoulders, much to Sam's annoyance.

"It's okay. You're going to be all right."

Sam's eyes widened, and her pulse raced. It was obvious, if only to her, that this damn woman was playing Bob; however, he was far too gullible to see it. Bethany was purposely making Sam out to be an ogre. She left the barn and bit down on her tongue so hard that a metallic taste filled her mouth. Sam surveyed the area, searching for possible food storage bins.

Seeing a blue container on the other side of the farmyard, she swooped to pick up a nearby bucket and marched over to check if it contained the pellets she had watched Bethany feed the pigs on an earlier visit. She opened the lid and found what she was looking for. After filling the bucket to the brim, she returned to the barn. Bethany was up on her feet now and saw her enter the barn with the food.

Sam sensed trouble and hurriedly threw the feed over the barrier into the pen.

"How dare you? That food is rationed. It costs a lot of money to keep the animals on this farm, and you come along and waste a bucketful on these creatures, when they've already been fed this morning."

The squealing in the barn died down, and the pigs grunted and barged each other out of the way, eager to get to the pellets.

"They're starving, any fool can see that, and that dead sow needs to be removed. We're not leaving until that's done and a vet has checked these animals and passed them fit. Make the call, Bethany, or I'm warning you, I'll ring the authorities and get this place closed down. The choice is yours."

"I'll ring the vet. Which one?" Bob jumped in, his phone in his hand ready to dial the number.

"It's in Workington."

"Which one?" Sam demanded, her patience waning rapidly.

"Animal Doctors, I think it's called. They've not been

open that long but they've been kind to us. The other ones in the area have ripped off the farmers for years."

Sam doubted if her statement was true. Bob left the barn and made the call. Sam could hear him explaining the situation to the receptionist.

He returned and said, "A vet will be here within half an hour."

"And who is going to pay for it?" Bethany screeched.

"You will. It's your responsibility to care for all the animals on this farm. You get a grant from the government, don't you?" Sam asked.

"It's a small one."

"I refuse to let animals suffer on my watch. Having a dead sow in the pen is distressing for the other pigs."

"You know bugger all. It's called nature," Bethany spat back at her.

"They've quietened down now because I took it upon myself to feed them. I might not be a farmer, but I know the basic needs required for healthy animals." Sam marched out of the barn and back to the car. She made a concerted effort to calm her breathing as she leant against the bonnet of her vehicle.

Bob left the barn with his arm around Bethany. Sam felt physically sick and had to swallow down the bile burning her throat after feeling betrayed by her partner. Bob saw Bethany to the front door of the farmhouse. She beamed at him, said thank you, then went inside the house, closing the door with a bang.

Bob joined Sam, and she could tell he was embarrassed.

"Don't start. I know you're angry with me, but it's not like you to be down on people, Sam. She's grieving, I don't suppose she's thinking straight right now, and by all accounts, Jenny has walked away and left her to fend for herself. That's a tough ask, when her husband and Mick have both died in the past week or so."

"No, you're wrong. You're forgetting a massive factor to do with this investigation, Bob."

"What's that?"

"Both men were *effing murdered*." It began to drizzle. Sam withdrew the sheet of paper from her pocket and sat in the car. She dialled the number and put it on speaker. "Hello, is this Greg?"

"Yep, who wants to know?"

"I'm Detective Inspector Sam Cobbs of the Cumbria Constabulary. I'm calling from Workington."

"Right, and?"

"I was hoping to speak with your sister, Jenny. Is she with you?"

"No, why? Should she be?"

Sam faced Bob and gave him a stick-that-in-your-pipe-and-smoke-it kind of look. "Umm... we're at the farm now, and your stepmother told us she was with you."

"She's a liar." His tone was icy cold.

"Are you telling me that she hasn't come to stay with you?"

"No. I haven't seen her for a couple of years. Furthermore, I wouldn't believe a thing that woman told you either. If you sliced her down the middle, she'd have *Evil Cow* running through her."

"I see. Have you spoken to your sister since your father passed away?"

"Yes. But only briefly. She was in shock and couldn't speak for long. Jenny was really close to my father. Is the bitch there? Bethany?"

"She's in the house. We're waiting for the vet to arrive."

"Why?"

"The pigs were distressed when we got here, so we've

rung the vet as a precaution. I think your stepmother is struggling to cope with running the farm."

"What about that bloke who works for them? Can't he put in some extra hours? Mark, is it?"

"Mick Bartlett. Sorry to be the bearer of bad news, but he also died last week."

"He what? No one told me. How?"

Sam heaved out a breath. "He was murdered."

"What the actual fuck, and now you're telling me that my sister has gone missing?"

"So it would seem. Bethany said she packed a bag and was heading your way."

"Jesus Christ. I've got a few days off work; I'll come back and help look for her."

"There's no need. I'm sure Jenny will turn up sooner or later."

"You reckon? Have you tried her mobile? Or been to the salon where she works?"

"She was due to return to the salon this morning. She failed to show up for her shift, hence the reason behind our visit today, and yes, we've tried ringing her mobile several times. It goes straight to answerphone."

"Bugger. Can't you trace her phone? Isn't that what you guys do, in cases such as this?"

"We're in the process of doing that at the moment," Sam fibbed and made a mental note to get in touch with Claire to organise the task. "Do you know anywhere else Jenny is likely to go? What about friends in the area?"

"I haven't got a clue. If that was the case, why would Bethany tell you she was coming to stay with me?"

"Okay. Any other family members in the area that we could try?"

"No one. You need to take Bethany in for questioning,

force the damn truth out of her. I'm going to pack a bag now. I can be there in a couple of hours."

"Please, if you're going to travel to the area, don't cause any trouble. Will you stay at the farm?"

"No. That woman and I have never seen eye to eye. I couldn't stay under the same roof as her."

"Okay. Is my number showing up on your phone?"

"Yes."

"Add it to your contacts and ring me as soon as you're settled somewhere."

"I'll do that." He hung up.

Sam cocked an eyebrow at Bob. "You still think I've got this all wrong?"

"Correct me if you disagree, but I've never said that. All I've been doing is advising you to take things easy on her. I don't have to remind you that you've already got a complaint hanging over your head, do I?"

"No, you don't, and how many of those have I had over the years?"

He placed a thumb and forefinger around his chin. "Let me think."

Sam prodded him in the leg with her outstretched fingers.

"Ouch. Okay, not many, if any."

"Thank you. Surely now you can see where this is leading? I think she put in an early complaint to keep us at bay."

"Truthfully?"

"Yep. Why else would she do it? All we've done so far is make general enquiries about her husband's death, nothing more. I've never accused her of doing anything wrong, have I?"

"No, not from what I can remember."

"So, why would an innocent person, with nothing to hide,

go to my senior officer and complain about how I've treated them? You heard what Greg said, she's evil."

"Maybe he was close to his mother and hated the thought of taking orders from Bethany. It must be difficult accepting another woman and to take orders from her. Is that why he took off?"

"True. But she's hardly proved herself to be meek and mild since we've been dealing with her, has she? No, she's always come across as feisty, up for a fight, right from the word go. Does that kind of behaviour go hand in hand with someone grieving the loss of their husband? No, it doesn't," she said, asking a couple of questions and answering them herself instead of giving her partner the opportunity to add his ten cents' worth.

Sam decided to call the station. "Claire, it's me. I need you to drop everything and carry out an urgent task for me."

"What's that, boss?"

"I need you to track Jenny Davidson's phone. We've been to the salon; she hasn't shown up for work. We're out at the farm, and according to her stepmother, she took off and is staying with her brother in Penrith."

"Don't tell me, you've contacted the brother and she's not with him either?"

"Spot on. I need you to find that phone, and quickly."

"You think something has happened to her?"

"Either someone has hurt her, or she's taken herself off the radar and is staying at a friend's or with a member of her family. Who knows what state of mind she's in after tragically losing her father?"

"Leave it with me. I'll get on it now and get straight back to you if I find anything."

"Cheers, Claire. We're staying out at the farm, awaiting the arrival of a vet. Don't ask, I'll fill you in when we get back. Quick question that I've failed to follow up with you for a few days, any news on Bethany's background?"

"Her bank account checks out, and so does her husband's. No large deposits or withdrawals made over the last couple of years."

"And her personal details?"

"I'm struggling to find anything before her marriage."

"Really? You mean under her previous name?"

"That's correct. I was beginning to wonder if there was still a glitch in the system."

"Keep trying. I need cold hard facts to throw at her rather than end up in the DCI's bad books again. We shouldn't be too long."

"See you later."

Sam jabbed the End Call button and faced her partner again. "Well? What do you make of that?"

He shrugged. "You tell me. You're the one who seems to have all the answers, not me."

"I don't want to fall out about this, Bob. A little support from you wouldn't go amiss, just saying."

"I am backing you up. I'm just adding the touch of caution that you usually have during an investigation. I know I keep coming back to the complaint issue…"

"Well, don't. I don't need to be reminded, it's firmly embedded in my mind and fuelling me enough as it is."

A Land Rover drew up alongside them.

"The vet has arrived," Bob stated the obvious with a grin.

"Your powers of deduction never cease to amaze me." Sam darted out of the car before Bethany noticed. She produced her ID and said, "DI Sam Cobbs. We made the call as we felt the animals were in severe distress."

The young male frowned. "I see, and is the farmer around? I'm Nicholas Sparks by the way."

"Pleased to meet you. Unfortunately, he died last week.

His wife is running the farm herself as their farmhand also died recently."

"Ah, yes. I remember hearing the sad news on the local radio. Is she around?"

"She's in the house."

With that, Bethany appeared and marched towards them, her arms pumping like pistons. "Before you go any further, I haven't called you out, so don't bother sending me the bill."

Nicholas opened the back door to get his bag out but paused. "Am I wasting my time here? If you're refusing to pay, I don't know what you expect from me."

"I'll pay," Sam said. "I just need you to check the animals are okay before I ring the authorities and put in a complaint about how they're being treated." *There's that word again! Take that, you evil cow.*

"Really? This is most unusual, Inspector," Nicholas said. "Are you sure you want to go down this route?"

"Absolutely. You'll understand for yourself when you see what awaits you in the barn, the one over there."

"You go in there and you'll never set foot on this farm again," Bethany warned. She folded her arms and tapped her foot.

The vet exchanged a concerned glance with Sam. She nodded, as if to say, 'See what I'm up against here?'

"I have a duty of care under the Animal Welfare Act, to investigate any form of neglect. That includes farm animals who are believed to be in distress."

Sam nodded and showed him into the barn. She pointed at the sow lying on the filthy bed of straw.

"Goodness me. I see what you mean. How long has this sow been dead?"

His question was directed at Bethany who had reluctantly followed them. "I don't know. I checked them first thing this morning, and everything was all right in here."

"When were the pigs last fed?" Nicholas asked.

"I fed them some pellets when we arrived, so about thirty minutes ago," Sam said. "The noise was deafening in here, they were squealing, going frantic. I was worried in case they started eating her. The babies are still trying to feed from her. I had to do something, I couldn't leave things the way they were."

He nodded. "You've done the right thing. Mrs Davidson, this was your responsibility, to feed them and to ensure there are no fatalities amongst the drove. You've clearly let your animals down. Is there someone else around who can help me remove the sow? We're going to need to round up the piglets, too, they'll have to be hand-reared unless you can get another sow to adopt them as her own."

"I haven't got time for this." Bethany snarled at Sam, "You called him, you can sort it out. I'll be up the top field, seeing to the cattle up there."

"Wait. No way, you can't leave us to deal with this," Sam objected, but the woman turned on her heel and scurried off in a huff.

"We'll do it," Bob said.

A tractor started up outside. Sam glared at Bethany who was sitting in the cab of the tractor. She scowled in response, which ultimately developed into a wicked smile before she headed off through a gate that led into one of the nearby fields.

"Are you sure about this? It's a mucky job," Nicholas warned them.

"We can put a suit on, can't we, partner? Do you want to collect a couple from the boot?"

Bob left the barn, and Sam approached the pen.

"It's horrendous. The woman shouldn't be left in charge of the animals if she's unable to tend to their basic needs."

"What about the farming community? They usually band

together and help out in cases such as this. I can't believe no one in the area has volunteered to assist her."

"I'm at a loss to know what to say. We've come here today to speak with her stepdaughter, only to find that she's also left the farm. Jenny is currently on the missing list as she hasn't arrived at her intended destination."

"Goodness me, it gets worse. That poor woman must be overwhelmed with grief, I'm not surprised the animals are being neglected."

Sam bit down on her tongue. Bob reappeared and passed her a suit which she stepped into. She jumped up and down to get the perfect fit. "Okay, where do you want us?"

Nicholas took off and searched the barn at the rear. He came back with a sack truck. "This will help. Pigs are heavy animals to move, but before we can shift the sow, we're going to need to round up the little ones first. They're wriggly creatures and squeal when touched, so be aware of that."

"Where shall we put them?" Sam asked, trepidation rising within.

"At the rear. There's another small area that's been fenced off back there. I need to know if she's going to bottle feed them or put another sow with them."

"Hopefully she'll be back soon. Once she's calmed down."

"If you can help me to get the sow out and the piglets settled into their new home, maybe I can make a few calls to some of the farmers nearby, ask them if they wouldn't mind lending Mrs Davidson a hand for a few days."

"Sounds like a great idea and would no doubt be better coming from you."

He held up his crossed fingers. "We'll see about that. I'm quite new to the area. They're just as likely to give me the finger and tell me to swivel on it. Oops, sorry, was that too rude to say out loud?"

Sam and Bob both laughed which eased the tension in the

barn. She liked this man. He reminded her a little of Vernon, her footballer brother-in-law.

It took the three of them nearly fifteen minutes to round up the ten piglets and to put them in the other pen, then Nicholas unhitched a length of the rail surrounding the other pigs, to secure them while they moved the dead sow.

They were nearing the end of the strength-sapping task when, in the distance, Sam noticed the sound of the tractor returning. Bethany appeared in the doorway once Nicholas had put the rail back and freed the other animals.

Sam walked over to Bethany. "All done. Where shall we put it?"

"I don't know, you tell me. Do I have to get rid of it? Or will you need to take it with you to carry out a necropsy?" she asked Nicholas.

"No, that'll cost money you can ill afford."

"But what if she's been deliberately killed, perhaps poisoned? My husband and his colleague have been murdered. What if someone is doing this to drive my business and livelihood into the ground?"

"It's possible, I suppose," Nicholas admitted. "The choice is yours."

"I won't pay for anything extra," Sam said, "only the vet's callout fee, Mrs Davidson, so the extra cost will fall on your shoulders."

"I'll give NFSCO a ring, they collect any fallen stock in the area," Nicholas informed them. "The closer we put it to the main entrance the better."

"Will they collect it today?" Bethany asked. "I don't relish that great lump lying in the farmyard all day or all week."

"They should collect it within a few hours at the maximum. I'll ring them now. There are a few other calls I need to make as well."

"You do that. Bob and I can finish shifting the pig with the aid of the sack truck."

Nicholas raised his eyebrow. "If you're sure?"

"We insist, don't we, partner?"

Bob stared at her. "If you say so."

Nicholas laughed. "I think your partner had other ideas, Inspector. Here, I can lend a hand getting the sow back on the truck. Once it's tipped back it'll be easier for you both to move, that is unless Mrs Davidson wants to give you a hand."

"I don't, I have a bad back at the best of times," Bethany was quick to retort.

By now, the three of them, were experts at the way a pig's body flopped. They managed to get the beast on the truck. Bethany stood by and let them take the strain which only succeeded in getting Sam's blood boiling again. Bethany drifted off without Sam realising it moments later.

"Where did she go?" Sam whispered, puffing and panting through their exertions.

"I think she went back to the farmhouse. I might be mistaken, though, I was otherwise engaged."

They deposited the sow close to the gate and removed their suits and gloves which Sam put in the bin near the house. She slapped her hands together, triumphant in their efforts.

"Well done us. When I initially felt the weight of it, I thought it was going to be an impossible task to fulfil."

Nicholas joined them and cast a look over his shoulder before he spoke. He lowered his voice and told them, "I've rung several of the farms in the area, and no one is willing to give the woman a helping hand."

Sam inclined her head and asked, "Ouch, did they say why?"

He peered over his shoulder once more and shrugged.

"They can't stand the woman. Apparently, she's been a thorn in the farming community's side since she married Alvin."

Sam nodded. "Wow, that's some statement. Okay, it's an unfortunate situation, but there's nothing legally we can do about it. We can't force people to do the right thing and offer to help in extreme circumstances."

"Believe me, I tried every trick in the book to shame them into changing their minds without overstepping the mark. It didn't wash with them."

"Never mind. You've done enough coming out here today and lending a hand. How much do we owe you?"

"It should be a hundred and fifty quid, but I'm willing to go halves with you, if it'll help?"

Sam took the hit on the chin. "Thanks, that's kind of you." She went back to the car to collect her purse. Luckily, she had drawn out some cash over the weekend and handed him the seventy-five pounds. "I'd say it's been a pleasure doing business with you, but I'd be lying," she said.

The three of them laughed.

Nicholas changed out of his suit and jumped back into the Land Rover. Sam waved him off and turned to her partner.

"What now?" she asked.

"You're the boss for a reason. Me, I could do with a pint down the pub after my exertions, but the prospect of that happening is negligible, isn't it?"

"Why bother suggesting it if you know what the answer is going to be?"

"Nothing wrong in chancing your arm now and again, is there?"

"Keep trying. You might strike lucky one day, just not today. I need to go into battle with Bethany."

"Christ, why? Can't you leave the woman alone for now?"

Sam frowned and shook her head. "No, I need to get her

reaction to the news that Jenny has possibly gone missing, or had you forgotten that morsel of information we gleaned before Sowgate struck?"

She could tell he was suppressing a smile, determined not to laugh at her quip. "You win, it's your call. Are you going to tell her that Greg is travelling down from Penrith?"

"Nope. She'll find out for herself soon enough. I want to see if that works in our favour."

It was Bob's turn to frown. "How?"

"You know how people tend to react when they're put under pressure. I could do with rattling her cage a touch and I think Greg is just the man to do that for us."

"Ha, and you think she's got an evil streak. I've got news for you, you're giving her a pretty good run for her money, I can assure you."

She grinned and headed towards the house, her heart pounding so hard she felt it vibrating against her ribs. Sam knocked on the door. It took Bethany a while, but she eventually answered it.

"Sorry to trouble you. I have some disturbing news for you that I discovered earlier, before the unfortunate incident with the sow."

Bethany folded her arms. "Oh, what joy, yet more disturbing news for me to deal with. Go on then, spit it out."

"You gave me Greg's number. When I rang him, he was surprised to learn that Jenny wasn't here at the farm."

Bethany's brow furrowed. "Wait, what are you telling me?"

"That Jenny never arrived at her brother's. We're going to have to take a statement from you, and you're going to need to file a missing person report."

"I am? Why? If the girl wants to take off and lie to me about where she's going, then what am I supposed to do about it? She's twenty-three, for God's sake, hardly in her teens."

"That's as may be, but there is still a genuine concern about her whereabouts, given the circumstances surrounding her father's and Mick's deaths."

"You think someone has taken her? Kidnapped her? For what? A possible ransom? Well, they'll be in for a shock if they think I have any money to hand over. I'm broke, barely surviving as it is."

"It's not something I'm willing to ignore. Are you going to work with me, us, or not?"

Bethany locked gazes with her and shrugged. "If you want. Do I have the option not to?"

"Of course, but it'll look bad on you if you refuse to assist us with our enquiries. Can we come in?"

"No, the place is a mess. I'm grieving still and haven't bothered to do an ounce of housework since Alvin died—sorry, was murdered. Maybe that's why Jenny has taken off. She's never been the type to get her hands dirty and help me keep the house clean."

"Okay, I'll get a statement from the car, and we can go over the details." Sam trotted back to the vehicle and removed a clipboard and form from the folder of paperwork she kept stored in there for such occasions, which thankfully wasn't called for that often. It was her least favourite part of the job, apart from dealing with the daily mail that blighted her life.

"Here we go. Let me just fill in the relevant details at the top and we'll get started. Right, now then, can you tell us what happened just before Jenny left?"

"Yes. At first, I assumed she was going into work as usual, but she had different ideas. She had an overnight bag on the floor beside her. When I asked her what was going on, she blurted out that she'd had enough of moping around and she was determined to get her life back on track. I queried what she meant by that statement. She said she hadn't seen Greg for a while and needed to be with him. To be honest with you, I was mortified that she was willing to leave me at this time. Not only do I have her father's funeral to arrange but I'm under the cosh around here as well. I called her selfish. She ignored me, ate her breakfast and left the house."

"What time was that?"

"Around eight forty-five, or thereabouts. I can't give you a definitive time because I had other things to consider, like feeding the pigs et cetera."

Sam glanced up from the statement, and they glared at each other for a few seconds.

"Did she take her car?"

"Yes, and don't bother asking me for the details. It's white, that's all I know. I have no interest in what make or model a car is, like every other woman I know."

"We can find out the information back at the station. And she hasn't contacted you since she left this morning?"

"No. I asked her to call me once she landed in Penrith, so to speak, but I've heard nothing from her at all. Of course, she might have rung while I was out feeding the animals. I don't make a habit of checking the phone for missed calls, as if I've got time for that."

"Even when Jenny is on the road?"

"Even then. As you can see, life around here is full-on most days."

"Is there anywhere else Jenny might have gone on the way to her brother's?"

"You tell me, because I don't know. I'm concerned she hasn't reached there by now, she's long overdue."

Sam glanced at her watch. It was almost two in the afternoon. "It does seem strange that she hasn't arrived there. It's even stranger that when I spoke with Greg earlier, he had no idea that she was on the way to stay with him. Why do you think that is?"

"I haven't got the foggiest. What are you insinuating, Inspector?"

"I'm trying to figure out what goes on in a young woman's mind who has recently lost her father."

"As if I'm likely to be aware of that. Family members grieve in different ways for a loved one who has passed. I've had to set my own grief aside for the moment because I have far too much going on around here to worry about. I'm upset she hasn't stuck around to give me a hand but what could I do? Insist she helps me? I'm not the type to force someone to do something against their will."

"I'm glad to hear it. Hopefully, she'll have forgotten to charge her phone and stopped off on the way, you know, to break up the journey."

"Yes, I'm sure you're right. Now, is there anything else? Only I have yet more animals to feed out in the fields."

"Bob, can you take some notes down for me, please?"

Bob withdrew his notebook and gave her a quizzical look.

"Perhaps you can give us the details of her friends, so we can check with them?" Sam said.

"I would if I could. All her contacts are in her phone. You know what youngsters are like with their mobiles, it's everything in the world they need. You might want to investigate people who have caused problems for her in the past."

"Do you have anyone in mind?"

"Yes, I made a note of three ex-boyfriends; they all parted on bad terms with Jenny. It's just a thought." She handed Sam a slip of paper.

Sam read the note, and it had three names and addresses written on it. Her mind whirling, she decided to leave the interview there. "Thanks for your help. Let's hope Jenny shows up soon, either comes back home or ends up with her brother."

"We live in hope. Is there anything else now?"

"No. We'll leave you to it. Oh no, one last thing. Do you have a gun on the premises?"

"Yes, Alvin had one, but it's locked in the cabinet, where it's always kept."

Bethany slammed the door shut in their faces. Sam hadn't been prepared for that and flinched as the draught hit her in the face.

"Come on, we've spent enough time around here today."

"Suits me. Any chance we can stop off for a pub lunch on the way back?"

"Are you buying? I'm seventy-five quid down on the day already."

"And whose fault is that?"

She stopped walking. "Are you telling me I did the wrong thing, calling the vet out? Because in case you missed it, he pretty much backed up my claims that Bethany had neglected her duties."

Bob sighed and rolled his eyes. "We're never going to agree on this one. She's grieving, Sam. She's got so much shit being flung at her, you need to put yourself in her shoes and see how you would cope if you ever found yourself in her position."

"I have news for you, partner, I've been there, or are you forgetting that fact?"

"Shit!" he mumbled.

Sam seethed as she continued her journey towards the car. She threw the clipboard on the back seat and slipped behind the steering wheel. Bob clipped his seat belt in place and muttered an apology.

"What are you apologising for? Talking bullshit or for not having my back during this investigation?"

"Both. I just thought you were coming down heavy on her when you shouldn't be, that's all."

"I'm not, not intentionally. I'm the lead investigator with two serious crimes to solve. The least you can do is give me your full support, Bob. I'm getting sick to death of tiptoeing around you."

"I apologise. I take it all back. If anything, I was looking out for you."

"Jesus, are you talking about the complaint again?"

"Yes."

"Well, stop harping on about it. I have no intention of changing the way I conduct an investigation, despite having that over my head. I'm an utter professional, in case that has escaped your notice lately."

"It hasn't."

"Right, let that be the end of it. I need food. Do you know of any decent pubs out this way or on the edge of town?"

"Not really. What about The Galloping Horse? You get a great meal there."

"The Galloping Horse it is then. One last thing regarding Bethany before we move on."

"Go on."

"Don't you think it's strange that she should have a list of ex-boyfriends to hand and yet couldn't supply the names of any of Jenny's friends?"

He fell quiet. Sam knew that meant that he was contemplating her question, giving it extra consideration before he replied.

"Okay, you've got me on that one."

Sam silently marked the air with her finger. *Gotcha! Hung, drawn and quartered. Get out of that one if you can, matey!*

CHAPTER 8

With lunch out of the way, which happened to be one of the nicest pub meals she'd had in a long time, they returned to the station.

Sam stopped at Claire's desk on the way to her office. "Any luck on Jenny's phone?"

"Sadly not, boss. It rang a couple of times, each time connecting with the answerphone, but when I've tried it recently, it's not even ringing, it's dead."

"And there's no way we can trace a dead signal, right?"

"Nope."

"Okay, do me a favour and keep ringing it periodically, just in case it's run out of charge and comes back online."

"Of course."

"I'll be in my office, should anyone need me." There, she took a moment to enjoy the view, her thoughts bouncing around, lots of questions cluttering her mind. Eventually, she forced herself to make the calls. Once settled behind her desk, she rang Scott, the first name on her list. His mobile rang four times. Sam was about to hang up, but he answered just in time.

"Mr Carl Scott?"

"Yes. And you are?"

"I'm DI Sam Cobbs of the Cumbria Constabulary. Do you have a moment for a quick chat?"

"I'm busy clearing up at the pub, what's this about?"

"Jenny Davidson."

"Well, that's a name from a dark and distant past. What about her? Has she broken the law?"

"No, not in the slightest. She's gone missing, and I'm in the process of going through her friend list," Sam replied, stretching the truth.

"I think you're mistaken. Jenny and I broke up about four years ago as sworn enemies, in her eyes, at least."

"Oh, can you tell me why you broke up?"

"I started seeing someone else... behind her back, and she found out about it."

"Ah, okay. And you work at a bar, did you say?"

"I run it. The Horse and Hounds in Workington."

"I think I know it. When was the last time you saw her?"

"About four years ago. She knows I run this place and steers clear of it."

"Okay, thanks for speaking with me. I'll let you get on. If you should happen to see her, will you call the station, let them know where she is?"

"Of course. I hope you find her soon."

Sam ended the call and put a tick by his name then scribbled down the relevant information he'd given her and moved on to the second name, Ben Dereham.

"Hello, is that Ben?"

"It is. Who's this?"

"Sorry to trouble you, Ben, I'm DI Sam Cobbs of the Cumbria Constabulary."

"The police. Oh right, what can I do for you, Inspector?"

"I'm making general enquiries, it's nothing to worry about as such."

"Enquiries about what?"

"Do you know Jenny Davidson?"

The line fell quiet.

"Hello, Ben, are you still there?"

"I am. Sorry, I haven't heard that name for a while."

"Have you either seen or heard from Jenny lately?"

"How lately? We broke up about three years ago. Actually, I can tell you now, I haven't seen her since we stopped going out together."

"May I ask why you split up?"

"Because she never had any spare time to spend with me. She worked at a salon during the day and helped out on her father's farm most nights."

"During the winter months?"

"I don't know if that's true or not. I started seeing her in June and ended the relationship two months later. I think we only went out a couple of times. I liked her, but I wanted more from a partner at the time."

"Thanks, that's very helpful."

"What's this all about?"

"Jenny has gone missing, and we're checking if any friends or acquaintances might have seen her."

He laughed. "I don't think she would call me a friend. I was narked when we split up. She just shrugged it off as if it were an everyday occurrence. I really liked her. But I wasn't prepared to put my life on hold while she worked for the family farm, and yes, I did volunteer to go over there and help out. She and her father laughed in my face. Told me farming wasn't for novices and there was a lot more involved than the general public realised."

"Okay, well, at least you tried."

"I did. I hope she shows up soon. Does the family still have the farm?"

"Yes. Unfortunately, Jenny's father passed away last week, which is why I'm more than a little concerned about her."

"Bugger. If there's anything I can do, just give me a shout."

"I will, thanks for speaking with me." Sam ended the call and rubbed at her temple. She had a feeling which direction the third call was going to take. *Come on, I need to push myself to do this.*

"Hello, are you Robin Edwards?"

"That's correct. How can I help?"

"I'm Detective Inspector Sam Cobbs from the Cumbria Constabulary. Do you have a moment to talk?"

"I do. You've caught me between customers."

"Oh, that's great. Where do you work?"

"I'm an insurance rep at an office in Workington. What can I do for you, Inspector?"

"Do you know Jenny Davidson?"

"I used to, but no longer."

"Am I right in thinking you used to date at one time?"

"We did. For about four months, no longer than that. Is everything okay with her? It's been years since we've seen each other. I don't tend to keep in touch with my exes."

"Here's the thing, she's been reported missing, and I'm in the process of ringing around people who knew her, to see if they might have either seen or heard from her over the last couple of days."

"Missing? That's a shame. I haven't had any contact with her in around two years. By missing, do you mean that something bad has happened to her?"

"I can neither confirm nor deny that at present because we just don't know. She was due to arrive at her brother's in Penrith and hasn't shown up there."

"What about her phone? Or am I asking the obvious here?"

"We're trying to trace it but we're not having much luck with that at this time, hence our concern for the young woman's safety."

"I'd love to help. I liked Jenny, I really did, except she seemed a little mixed up when I was dating her, and she refused to open up to me."

"Interesting. Do you think she had problems at home?"

"Yes, although she wouldn't tell me exactly what was going on. I think her father was all right towards her, in fact, I believe they are really close. I think the problem lies with that evil stepmother of hers."

"Evil? Can I ask why you chose to call her that?"

"Because she was, from what I can remember. She definitely ruled the household. According to Jenny, she had to run everything past the woman. I told her to get a flat of her own, but she said she feared what would happen to her father if she left the farm. In the end, I felt she was really down, and I couldn't handle the stress. If she wasn't bothered about changing the situation she was in, then there was little point in us continuing our relationship."

"I understand. Is there anything else you'd like to add? Any strange incidences that occurred up at the farm when you were there perhaps?"

"Let me think about that for a moment. No, I don't think so. I believe I only visited the place a couple of times. Never felt comfortable under that woman's scrutiny."

"Just to clarify, are you talking about Bethany?"

"That's right, the evil stepmother. Jenny also called her that by the way."

"Did she? When I've spoken to them together, I've always got the impression they liked one another. Thanks for the insight." But it also made her remember part of the conversation she'd had with Bethany before when she had challenged Jenny with, *'If you have something to say, my girl, let's hear it.'*

"You're welcome. Was there anything else I can help you with? Only I'm due to see another customer in five minutes and I have to prepare the paperwork for the appointment."

"No, that's all. I can't thank you enough for speaking with me today. It's been a huge help."

She replaced the phone in its docking station and ran a hand around her face. A knock sounded on the door, and Bob poked his head around it.

"Hey, what's up?"

"You've got a visitor downstairs who wants to see you."

Sam frowned. "Do they have a name?"

"It's Greg Davidson. He's pretty annoyed."

"Okay. I've just rung the three ex-boyfriends. The last one I spoke to gave me an insight into the relationship between Jenny and Bethany, and it isn't a good one."

"Backing up your thoughts about the woman, right?"

"Yep. There's more to her than meets the eye. Get Claire to up the ante on sourcing the background information about her and, while I go downstairs and speak with Greg, can you see if there are any life insurance policies for the couple?"

Bob tapped the side of his nose and winked. "I'm with you. Yep, I'll action that now."

Sam felt the need to take a few seconds to prepare herself for her meeting with Greg. She took a sip of water from the bottle on her desk and ran a comb through her hair, wincing as it hit a knot at the back. "Damn wind has a lot to answer for at this time of the year. Right, let's see what this young man has to say."

Raised voices coming from the reception area as Sam descended the stairs caught her on the hop. She upped her pace and pushed open the security door to find a young man,

TO BELIEVE THE TRUTH

she presumed to be Greg, being held by two uniformed officers.

"What's going on here?"

"Sorry, ma'am. Mr Davidson here was getting anxious, and it escalated quickly."

"Greg, I'm DI Sam Cobbs. We spoke on the phone earlier. I wasn't expecting you to show up here. I told you to contact me when you arrived in the area."

"Well, I thought I'd come and see you instead."

"Is the family room free, Sergeant?"

"Yes, ma'am. I'll get you the key."

Sam approached the desk and collected the key then turned to Greg and said, "If I ask the officers to let you go, are you going to behave yourself?"

He nodded. "You have my word. I didn't really do anything."

"We don't put up with people who have behavioural issues. Now, are you going to calm down and speak to me properly?"

"Yes. I promise."

"Follow me then. We'll have a quiet chat. Can I get you a drink?"

"Yeah, coffee, milk with one sugar would be great, thanks."

"Can you organise that for me, Sergeant?"

"I can. I'll bring it through. Do you want one of my officers to accompany you, ma'am?"

"Is there any need for that, Greg?"

"No. I'm sorry, I'm just concerned about my sister."

"I have news for you, we all are. Kicking off like that isn't going to help the situation, is it? Come with me. No, I've got this, Sergeant, thanks."

Greg retrieved his holdall from the seating area and followed Sam into the room off to the right. Nick brought

157

two cups of coffee in a few seconds later and closed the door behind him.

"I've been out there... to the farm. The bitch wouldn't let me in the house."

"I visited the farm myself earlier. There was an issue with one of the pigs. When my partner and I left, Bethany wasn't in the best of moods. I suppose you showing up only made matters worse. Did she speak to you?"

"Yeah, two words, one of them was *off*."

Sam grinned. "Sounds about right. I suppose in the circumstances we need to make exceptions for her foul mood."

"You might want to do that, but I shouldn't have to. That place used to be my family home until she came along. She's got no right slamming the door in my face, refusing me entry."

Sam sighed and shrugged. "Actually, she has. It's just something you're going to have to accept, for now."

"The woman drove me out of the house. She had one intention when she married Dad."

"And what was that?"

"To get her hands on that farm. It's worth a pretty penny, and now she'll be the one who inherits it all."

"It depends on what your father put in his will, surely."

"Will it? Won't it automatically go straight to her?"

"It might be worth us checking with the family solicitor. It's not something we've had a chance to delve into as yet."

"Why not? It should have been the first place you searched for clues. Maybe if you had, Jenny would still be around today. Where is she? What do you know about her disappearance?"

"Nothing so far, only what Bethany told us. She set off to see you in Penrith, she had a bag packed, ready for her visit."

"You've only got her word for that, haven't you? Have you traced her phone yet? Found her car on the ANPR system?"

Sam smiled. "You seem to be up to date with your police procedures. May I ask how?"

"I watch a lot of true crime shows on TV. They go through a lot of the procedural aspects to a case."

"So I've been told. Most of them are filmed in the States and they have a different way of policing over there, something for you to bear in mind."

"The basics are the same, aren't they?"

"Anyway, we're veering off track here. We're going to need to put our heads together to see if we can figure out where Jenny has gone. Bethany gave me the names of three of her ex-boyfriends. I've just come off the phone from speaking to them, and none of them have laid eyes on her for years."

"What about her close friends, have you tried them?"

"No, because we haven't been given that information."

His brow knitted. "What?"

"Precisely. If we haven't got the information, it kind of puts a kibosh on the enquiries we need to make."

"I get that. Why the boyfriends' details and not the friends'?"

Sam shrugged. "You tell me. Every turn we make seems to lead us into an area full of questions and very few answers."

"And it all stems from that bitch up at the farm, right?"

Sam raised her hands. "At this stage, I'm trying not to make any rash decisions."

"In the meantime, my sister is out there, who knows where, a frantic and screwed-up mess. Dad meant the world to her. You don't think she's run off with the intention of doing harm to herself, do you?"

"It's hard to say. I've only met Jenny recently, not long after she heard the news about her father. Understandably, she was very upset. Who knows what was going through that head of hers?"

"Strange question, has the funeral been arranged yet?"

"There was a hold put on it while the post-mortem was carried out. I'm not sure what the position is right now. I can call the pathologist, see what he can tell me."

"It might be worth it. If the funeral arrangements are underway then there would be no reason for Jenny to go AWOL. She'd be anxious to say her farewell to our father, nothing would stand in the way of her doing that."

Nothing or no one? What if Bethany tried to stand in her way? What if Jenny finally found her voice after being suppressed all these years and spoke out...? No, I can't go there, not yet, not without the evidence to back up such a claim.

"Inspector? Are you still with me?"

"Sorry, lost in a world of my own, revisiting the information we've gleaned so far about the case. I'll ring the pathologist. Give me a second." She left the room and rang the lab, only to be told that Des was in the middle of a PM and couldn't come to the phone. Sam requested that he ring her as soon as he became available as it was a matter of life and death. Overly dramatic maybe, but who's to say that wasn't the truth?

She returned to the room to find Greg looking thoughtful. "Any luck?" he asked.

"He's going to get back to me, he's performing a PM at the moment. Where will you stay while you're here?"

"I'll find a local Air B and B rather than a hotel to keep the cost down."

"May I suggest you don't venture out to the farm again? It's not worth it. Let us make the necessary enquiries and see what we can come up with. I don't suppose you know which solicitor your father used, do you?"

"Now you're asking. Sorry, nothing is coming to mind.

It's not the type of thing he ever discussed with me. It'll probably be someone local, knowing the way he always liked to work."

"That'll help narrow it down, thanks."

"What can I do while I'm here?"

Sam smiled, took a sip of her drink and said, "Keep your head down."

"Are you saying it's a waste of time me being here?"

"Possibly. Investigations as complex as this take time to solve. We have a few avenues we're pursuing right now, and until anything concrete comes back from them, we just need to tamp down our impatience."

"What about the farm? You mentioned that there was an issue there this morning. Can you tell me what it was?"

"We showed up, looking for Jenny, and the pigs were squealing. They hadn't been fed, and Bethany refused to see to them. I took it upon myself to feed them and discovered one of the sows had died. Maybe pigs are sensitive animals and the death was the problem, not the fact that they hadn't been fed for a while."

"I should imagine it was a mixture of both. Not that I profess to be a pig expert."

"Anyway, I called a vet out. We got the sow shifted ready for collection, but Bethany refused to cover the cost of the vet. I had to stump up with the cash."

"Stupid bloody woman, she has no idea how to run that place. I would volunteer to give her a hand, but I know she would probably sling it back in my face. She's the most unreasonable woman I've ever met. What Dad ever saw in her is beyond me."

"We're having trouble digging into her past, you know, as part of our ongoing enquiries. Is there anything you can tell us about her background?"

"Such as?"

"We've failed to find anything so far."

"Oh right. She was married before to a Colin Pullman; I think he was called that."

"Where did she live, in Cumbria?"

"No, down south, I think from the Bristol area. No kids. She said she never wanted them. Her husband died of a heart attack, at least that's what she told us."

Sam removed her notebook from her pocket and made a note of the details he was sharing with her. "Interesting. Why move to the area, any idea?"

"I'm not sure. I think they moved up here while her husband was alive, but that part is a bit sketchy."

"You're doing well. What about family? Can you tell me about them?"

"Not really, other than she came from a broken home, raised by her mother. She died quite young, I think when Bethany was in her teens."

"Siblings?"

"Not that I know of... no, wait, she mentioned, or let it slip once, that she had a baby sister, but she died when she was quite young. Cot death, maybe, I can't truly remember."

"That's brilliant. You've given us more than we've managed to obtain. Will you find a B and B now?"

"Yeah. You have my number. If I can assist you while I'm here, I'm willing to do it. Sorry for kicking off in the reception area, I'm really worried about my sister. There's no reason for her to take off, she's always been a home bird. Never had a holiday, as such, away from the farm. I think if Bethany hadn't come along when she had, Jenny would have stepped up to the plate and become a partner in the business with Dad. She thinks the world of the animals and loves caring for them. It was Bethany who insisted she become an apprentice stylist. Don't get me wrong, she's good at it and has even won several awards over the years, but her heart belongs with the farm, with the animals."

"I'm intrigued to know how they met, your father and Bethany."

"It was on one of those 'find a footloose and fancy-free farmer' dating sites. We warned Dad about going on that bloody site. I've never had to sink that low."

Sam shrugged. "Each to their own. I've heard several success stories over the years, not every site is a waste of time."

"Whatever. They met on the Friday, went out on a date, and she was moving her stuff into the farm the following week."

"Wow, that was quick work."

"The line they told us was that Bethany was being asked to move out of her rental property for the summer season and she had nowhere else to go. To be fair, she started off in the box room but ended up in the main bedroom after a couple of weeks. She was quite nice when she first came to the farm, but once she got her feet under the table, it was a different story. They got married after three months. That was a shock. I never thought Dad would ever take the plunge, not after losing Mum. They were genuinely devoted to each other. I suppose raising two teenagers finally took its toll on him and he welcomed the first woman who had shown interest in him in years, even if it was through one of those sites. I guess it depends on the level of desperation you need to sink to…"

"You're talking about inviting Bethany into the home, not desperation of using the site in the first place?"

"Either one. I wouldn't be seen dead trying to pick up a bird by flicking right, or is it left? See, I don't even know that."

"I have a confession to make, neither do I." She smiled.

"Okay, you've given us some valuable information that will hopefully open up another avenue of leads."

"Are you any further forward in the investigation? Do you know who killed my father?"

"Not really. During the initial stages it's all about the information we can gather and seeing where it leads us." *Maybe he hasn't twigged that I've been asking all these questions about Bethany because I believe she's our number one suspect. Maybe the penny will drop once he leaves the station.* "Take care of yourself. We'll keep in touch and, for everyone's sake, please stay away from the farm, especially as emotions are running high at the moment."

"I will. Thanks for seeing me at short notice. I appreciate how busy you must be, working two murder investigations plus looking for my sister. While I'm here, I'll visit some of her old haunts, make some enquiries of my own."

"You do that. If you find out anything, give me a shout."

They left the room, and Sam opened the main door for him. She shook his hand.

He held it longer than necessary and asked, "Do you think she's still alive?"

"Goodness, yes, of course I do. She's going through a traumatic time. Maybe she just needed a few days away to clear her thoughts."

"I hope you're right, however, my gut is telling me otherwise."

"Try and remain positive, that's all we can do."

She stood with the door open, the rain lashing her face, and watched him jog back to his car. Once he'd driven out of the car park, she went back inside and climbed the stairs to the incident room. Claire glanced her way, and Sam crossed the room to speak with her.

"Anything new?"

"No, not really."

"Okay, I've gathered some vital information from the stepson that I would like you to corroborate for me." Sam showed Claire the details she'd written in her notebook.

"Interesting indeed. Okay, at least it's given us something to work on. I'll get on it now."

"Great, I was hoping you'd say that."

"I'm in the process of trying to contact all the solicitors in the area and not having much joy yet," Bob shouted to gain her attention.

"Keep trying. Can you also contact the ones in Whitehaven as well?"

"Will do. How was Greg? Word has it he was kicking off downstairs."

"Nah, I talked him around. I have a way of calming people down."

Her partner rolled his eyes. "If you say so."

Sam turned her back on him and smiled. "Has anyone else got anything for me?"

Oliver raised a hesitant hand, and she walked towards his desk.

"You have?"

"I know you didn't ask me to, but I checked the ANPRs for Jenny's car and haven't managed to locate it at all."

"Hmm... not the news I was expecting to hear. Thanks for taking the task on. Can you keep checking, Oliver?"

"In all honesty, boss, I think something would have shown up by now, especially as there is only one possible route she could have taken to leave the farm."

She contemplated his answer for a few seconds. "Is there a possibility she could still be there, at the farm? What are we looking at here? Bethany refused to let us in the house, insisted that we should hold our conversation on the doorstep. What do you think about this news, Bob? You're the one coming down heavily on me for not giving Mrs

Davidson, or the Weeping Widow as I prefer to call her, the benefit of the doubt."

"I don't know. Might be worth checking it out."

"Oliver, can you organise a search warrant for the premises? I'm getting an ominous feeling about this case, and I've never fully trusted anything that woman has told us."

"I'll get on to them now, boss."

THE TEAM WORKED HARD for the rest of their shift, putting in a couple of extra hours at the end of it.

At eight, Sam decided they should call it a day. "Come on, guys. We've all worked our socks off today. Let's go home and get some rest and crack on with it again in the morning."

They didn't need telling twice. Everyone switched off their computer and tidied up their desk before they headed home for the evening.

"Any DIY plans for when you get home?" Sam asked Bob as they left the station a few minutes later.

"Nope, thank goodness. I can chill with a beer and watch a movie tonight, if Abigail is up for it. What about you?"

"Hopefully, Rhys will spoil me rotten with a sumptuous home-cooked meal of superb quality. Did I mention what an excellent chef he is?"

"No, go on, rub it in. Abigail does her best, but I wouldn't ever use the word *sumptuous* to describe any of her offerings."

Sam tipped her head back and laughed. "I hope you have the common sense not to criticise her attempts."

"Of course I don't, what do you take me for? My efforts have been pretty inedible over the years. Don't drop me in it with Abigail, will you? She does her best, and I appreciate it. You still won't hear me raving about the meals she serves me every night, though, just saying."

"There's an answer to that."

"I knew you'd come down on her side, that's why I've never mentioned it before."

"I dispute that, I'm not coming down on her side. What I was going to suggest before you rudely interrupted me was, why don't you both attend a weekend away at a cookery school? I've heard they can be a lot of fun."

Surprisingly, he didn't dismiss the idea the way she thought he would.

"Actually, that's not a bad suggestion. We could do with going away for a weekend and spending time together."

"Christ, I was only joking, but whatever works for you."

Four uniformed officers came tearing out of the station behind them and almost knocked Sam off her feet.

"Hey, slow down, where's the damn fire?"

"Sorry, ma'am. We're in a hurry, we've had a call to attend a disturbance up at the Davidsons' farm," one of the older officers informed them.

"What type of disturbance?"

"Mrs Davidson told us her stepson was up there, making a nuisance of himself."

Sam glanced at Bob. "Are you up for it?"

He shrugged. "Why not? I don't suppose my meal will taste any different to normal, maybe slightly more charred from sitting in the oven for an extra couple of hours. I might even stop off for fish and chips on the way home."

"Get in. I'll drive, unless you want to take your own car?"

"I'll take mine, that way I can go straight home."

"You go on ahead," Sam told the uniformed officers. "We'll be right behind you." It was an intentional ploy on her part. She was dying to see Bethany's reaction when she and Bob showed up, along with the patrol cars.

"I know what you're up to," Bob muttered as they raced towards their vehicles.

"Me? Just doing the Force a favour at the end of my shift, matey, that's all."

He glanced up at the starry night sky and pointed. "Oh, look, that little piggy has an extra set of wings, fancy that."

Sam laughed and slipped behind the steering wheel of her car. Once the convoy had left the station, she switched on her blues and twos, and the other vehicles followed suit.

They arrived at the farm to find Greg and Bethany having a very heated discussion on the doorstep of the farmhouse. Sam tore out of the car and approached the warring pair.

"Keep him away from me," a tearful Bethany shouted.

"I came here to discuss my sister's disappearance, and she just let rip at me," Greg said, his gaze seeking out Sam's.

Her stomach churning, she stood between the two of them. "Why don't we go inside and discuss this like civilised human beings?"

"He's not setting foot in this property. He made his choice to leave it years ago, causing untold damage to this family. Now he has the audacity to storm back in here, demanding all sorts. I've told him what he needs to know, it was the same thing I told you: Jenny left here this morning and, as far as I'm concerned, she was on her way to Penrith."

"You're a lying *bitch*. You've got what you wanted, driven us both away, so you could get your hands on this farm if anything ever happened to my father. It wouldn't surprise me if you killed him."

Silence filled the air, and Bethany's mouth dropped open. She shook her head, slowly at first, but it soon gained momentum. "How dare you? I want him off this land. He's trespassing, you need to arrest him. He's always had it in for me, since the day I moved in and took his mother's place."

"Ha, think again, *bitch*. Our mother was a special lady. You could never, not in your wildest dreams, ever come close to taking her place."

TO BELIEVE THE TRUTH

Bethany pointed her finger and aimed it at his chest. "I've got news for you, your father thought differently. I was the love of his life, *not* your mother. Now get off my land."

Two officers sensed Greg was about to strike and latched on to his arms.

"You heartless bitch. You've never cared about Jenny or me, not one sodding iota."

"That's a terrible thing to say." Tears flowed, and Bethany sniffled. "I've always gone out of my way for you kids. If your father was with us today, he'd back me up on that. It was you who rejected me, not the other way around." She stumbled against the doorframe.

Sam saw this as her opportunity to get inside the house. "Let me help you, Bethany. Come on, let me take you inside."

Bethany snatched her arm away and glared at Sam. "No, no one is coming in. I deserve my privacy. I'm mourning the loss of my loving husband. Do your job and get him away from here. I want you to make a note of this back at the station: if he comes here again, you should arrest him. He's deliberately trying to cause trouble for me at a time when my life has imploded. Have a heart, all of you. Do the right thing and let me grieve in peace."

Greg slow clapped her outburst. "And the Oscar goes to the grieving widow who has, up to now, successfully deceived the cops over the matter of her husband's death."

"You see the sarcasm I have to contend with? He's always been the same. His father couldn't stand the hassle and breathed a sigh of relief when Greg left the farm. Even though it meant extra work for Alvin, the peace and quiet that followed his departure was a blessing, for all of us, even Jenny would vouch for that, if she'd bothered to stick around. She's another one who has deserted a sinking ship. I'm struggling to run this farm on my own, and neither of them gives a damn."

"Don't listen to her. Why is she blocking you from entering the farmhouse? I'll tell you why, because Jenny is still in there. I bet this witch has got her trussed up in her bedroom," Greg shouted.

Sam's gaze drifted between Greg and Bethany. She tried to judge the woman's reaction to the accusation and found it impossible to figure out what was going on in the woman's head. Which surprised her. Over the years she'd become somewhat adept, some might say an expert, on how people behaved in certain situations. Not Bethany. Sam had always found her to be unreadable.

"There's a simple way to dispute such a claim. Will you let me check the house for his sister, Bethany?" Sam tried to call the woman's bluff.

Bethany folded her arms and glowered at Sam. "No. Get a warrant, that's the only way you'll get in this house."

"Very well, I'll get that arranged. Now, by saying that, all you've done is raise our suspicions. If you have nothing to hide you would let us in."

"Think what you like. You've had it in for me from day one, that's why I put in a complaint about you. Be careful, Inspector. A woman scorned…"

"Oh, I'll be careful all right. I'll get the warrant and do things according to the book. We will get to the bottom of why you're refusing us access to your property."

Bethany smiled, shrugged then entered the house and did her usual trick of slamming the door behind her.

Screw you, bitch. I'll be back here as soon as I have that warrant in my hand.

"You've really pushed the boat out this time," Bob muttered on the way back to the car.

"And you can wind your neck in. Jesus, instead of dishing out the clichés, here's one for you: she's really managed to pull the wool over your eyes, hasn't she?"

"Nope, not at all. I'm just saying that you're guilty of letting your feelings get the better of you, Sam. You're allowing her to get under your skin, why?"

"I don't know why. But she's not as innocent as you believe her to be, Bob, why can't you see that?"

They reached the patrol car.

Sam opened the back door to speak with Greg. "Why come here? After I strictly asked you to leave well alone?"

"I couldn't sit around doing nothing all night. My sister is missing, and she knows more than she's letting on. Why won't you believe me?"

"We have to take things slowly. A warrant has already been requested. Our hands are tied until we have that in our sweaty palms. You're either going to have to be patient with us or I'll have no alternative but to bang you up in a cell to prevent you from perverting the course of justice."

"You're kidding me, right?"

Sam shook her head. "No, I'm deadly serious. You need to back off and leave the investigation to us. We have procedures to follow, we can't raid the farmhouse willy-nilly, if that's what you think we should do. She has rights. We've applied for the necessary paperwork. The second I have that in my possession, we'll be here, in force, I promise you."

Greg's chin dipped to his chest. "I apologise. I've been foolish, I can see that now." His head rose, and he looked her in the eye once more. "But surely you can understand the depths of my frustration?"

"I can, believe me. I feel exactly the same way, but if we don't do things by the book, there's only going to be one winner, her. Trust me, I won't let you down. My team and I have invested a lot of blood, sweat and tears in this investigation, to mess up at this stage. These things have a habit of going the course, taking longer than usual to sort out. She'll be wary from now on, I can guarantee that. She knows we have her on our radar. Let's hold fire for a day or two and see if she messes up, okay?"

"A few days? I can't do it, Inspector, not when Jenny's life is probably in danger."

"You're going to have to. If you disrupt the investigation further, then I will have no other option but to arrest you. Am I making myself clear here?"

"Yes, perfectly. Can I go now?"

"Where?"

"Back to the guest house. I promise."

"Then yes, you're free to go, if you give me your word that I can trust you."

"You can, I swear."

"Then enjoy the rest of your evening, Mr Davidson." Sam spoke to the officers standing alongside her. "He's free to go, but make sure you escort him back to his B and B. Good evening, sir."

Greg got out of the car and crossed the farmyard to get into his own vehicle.

Sam watched him go with Bob breathing heavily beside her. "Let's hear it. You've obviously got something on your mind."

"Me? No way, I'm not about to cross that line again. I value my balls, and so does my wife. I prefer to get home every night with as few bite marks in them as possible."

Sam laughed and swiped his arm. The two patrol cars and Greg left the farmyard.

Sam returned to her car and shouted, "See you in the morning, bright and early. You first, I have a call to make before I leave."

He narrowed his eyes. "Really?"

"Yes, you go ahead. Trust me."

"If you insist. Stay safe, Sam."

"You worry too much."

TO BELIEVE THE TRUTH

"What can I say? I'm a born worrier where you're concerned. Over the last couple of years, you've attracted your fair share of problems."

"Get out of here." She laughed and dropped into the driver's seat. Then, her gaze drawn to her rear-view mirror, keeping a watchful eye on the farmhouse, she rang Rhys. "Hi, it's me. I'm on my way, I should only be fifteen minutes. Do you need me to pick anything up?"

"No, just come straight home. I've already walked the dogs, so you don't even have to do that when you get back."

"You're an absolute angel. See you soon."

She ended the call as the door to the farmhouse opened. She watched on as Bethany left the house and made her way over to the barn. Sam resisted the temptation to get out of the car and speak to her. Instead, she turned the key in the ignition and left the farmyard.

She drove back to the cottage, gripping the steering wheel tightly. Bob was right, she was guilty of letting the woman wind her up. Why? Because there was something in her eyes Sam didn't trust.

The dogs welcomed her with squeals of delight and lots of kisses that went a long way to brightening up her day. She cherished her time at home with Rhys and her adorable pooches. Over dinner, which was a delicious Thai green chicken curry, she let the day's pent-up feelings drift into oblivion.

Once they had cleared up the kitchen and were settled on the sofa, sipping a glass of wine, Rhys said, "You were late tonight. Dare I ask why?"

"The investigation took another sinister turn today."

"In what way?"

"The daughter of the first victim has gone missing. We visited the wife at the farm, Jenny's stepmother, and she told us that Jenny had taken off early this morning to visit her brother. I rang him. She hadn't arrived. Furthermore, he knew nothing about her intended visit. Then, this afternoon, he showed up at the station and kicked off. Despite thinking that I'd calmed him down, when Bob and I were leaving the station, four officers barged past us on the way out to the farm. I couldn't leave it there, I had to find out for myself what was going on over there. It was either that or receive a call later that would have disrupted our evening."

"Ah, I understand now. So, you drove out to the farm, and?"

"Greg and Bethany were at each other's throats, metaphorically speaking. It was getting heated, and I had to intervene and pull Greg away. Bethany is doing her best to make a fool out of us, as a Force, I just know it."

"If you feel like that then why don't you arrest her?"

"For what? Being a grieving widow? We haven't got anything against her, no clues or evidence as such. But she has something over me."

Rhys tutted and blew out a breath. "The complaint. Is that why you don't trust her?"

"Maybe. There's more to the woman than meets the eye. I've never dealt with someone so manipulative without being obvious about it, if that makes sense."

"A narcissist?"

"Yes, one hundred percent correct. The trouble is, my partner, the sweet endearing Bob, can't see it."

"Maybe it's a female thing. Perhaps you're far more perceptive than your partner and that's why you're an inspector and he's still a sergeant."

"Possibly. But it's causing unnecessary friction between us."

"Ouch, is it repairable?"

"I hope so. I would hate for either one of us to end up

with egg on the face, but it looks like that's on the cards. I'm praying it won't be me."

"Maybe Bob is being extra cautious, watching your back, with this complaint hanging over your head."

She took a sip of wine and leaned her head on his chest. "That's what I admire most about you, you always see the best in people."

He kissed the top of her head. "Not always, but most of the time."

"Come on, let's forget about watching TV tonight, I could do with an early night."

"You go up, I'll see to the dogs."

"Are you sure? I could do with having a shower."

"Go, do it. The smell of pigs is lingering in your hair."

"I'm not surprised, I haven't even told you the best part. It can wait."

They shared a kiss, and Sam ran up the stairs to rid herself of the day's trials and tribulations.

CHAPTER 9

The team continued to collate all the information they needed about Bethany Davidson. Claire worked miracles now the system was back up and running to its full potential. She discovered that Bethany's first husband hadn't had a heart attack after all, he'd died of suspicious circumstances. According to Bethany's statement, she had been out for the evening with friends and came home to find her husband dead in his chair. He'd been beaten to death with a crowbar in a suspected break-in. The window in the kitchen door had been broken, and the weapon was lying on the floor beside her husband.

The police had interviewed Bethany. She had been distraught throughout. Her alibi held firm, and forensics hadn't found any fingerprints on the weapon, meaning the killer had probably worn a pair of gloves. The coroner had filed it as a suspicious death. If that was the case, why had she told Greg and probably the rest of the family that her husband had died of a heart attack?

"Strange, right?" Bob whispered in her ear.

"Not strange at all. It's what I've come to expect from her, you just can't see it, can you?"

"Nothing to see in my eyes, although that snippet of information might be causing a little doubt to creep in."

"Hallelujah! It's about bloody time."

His eyes widened, and he tutted. "All right, no need to go over the top."

"Isn't there? When are you going to learn to trust my woman's intuition?"

"If there is such a thing, when Hell freezes over."

Sam glared at him. "Right, Claire, can you go back even further for me? Check out what happened to her parents. She also mentioned to Greg that she had lost a sibling."

"Strewth! You can't be serious?" Bob asked, his frustration evident in his tone.

"What? Of course. Who knows what the bloody woman is capable of?"

He shook his head and returned to his seat.

Sam walked into her office to find her phone ringing. "Hello, DI Sam Cobbs, how can I help?"

"I hope so. I think I've got the right person. Please, you have to help me."

"Hold on, try to remain calm. Who are you first of all?"

"Sorry, I'm so worried. I'm Holly Medina."

"Hello, Holly. Do I know you?"

"No, but the other day you spoke to my boyfriend. He told me you'd rung him about one of his exes, Jenny Davidson."

"Yes, I recall. I rang three people that day. Which one is your boyfriend?"

"Sorry, my head is so messed up, I'm not thinking straight. Carl Scott."

"Okay, is Carl all right?"

"You tell me. He's gone missing, and I don't know what to do about it."

"When did you last have any contact with him?"

"This morning. He was due to join me in town for a coffee, he never lets me down. He didn't show up. I've got an awful feeling lurking in the pit of my stomach that I can't shift."

"Have you tried ringing him?"

"Yes, his mobile rang for a few times then went dead. He always keeps it fully charged, he has to because of running the bar. I'm scared something bad has happened to him, Inspector. Please, will you help me?"

"I'll do my best. I'll get a patrol car to come out. You can give them a statement and log him as a missing person."

"Is that it? Can't you personally help me?"

"I'm sorry, I have two murders as well as a missing person case to investigate. My team is stretched to the limits."

The phone went dead.

Sam held it away from her and stared at it. "Charming. I can't be at everyone's beck and call." She replaced the phone and then thought better of it and picked it up again to dial the reception area. "Nick, it's DI Sam Cobbs. I've been on the phone with a Holly Medina, we got cut off. Actually, I think she hung up on me. Did you pass her through to me?"

"Yes, that's right, ma'am. Sorry, I should have had a word with you first, but a woman needed my help in reception and…"

"It's okay. Have you got her details?"

"I have them here."

"Okay, she's obviously distraught. Can you get a car over there and get a statement from her? We've got our backs against the wall, being involved with three investigations. I tried to tell her that, and she hung up on me. Can you deal with it for me?"

"Of course. I'll get someone over there right away."

"Thanks, you're a lifesaver. I never want to let anyone down, not if I can help it. But, as a team, we can't take anything else on at the moment, even if there is a tenuous link to our investigation. Shit! No, forget I said that. I'll send a couple of my guys over there to have a chat with her."

He laughed. "As you wish, ma'am. You're still going to need her details, aren't you?"

"You read my mind."

He gave her Holly's address. She hung up and immediately went back into the outer office. "Oliver and Alex, I know we're up against it, but humour me. I've had a call from Holly Medina, she's the girlfriend of one of Jenny's ex-boyfriends, Carl Scott. She rang me asking for help. Carl has gone missing, and she's frantic. It's unlike him not to show up when they've arranged a coffee date. She's tried calling his phone and it's dead. Again, she told me that never happens, he's anal about charging it fully every night because of the business he runs."

"Okay, what do you need us to do, boss?" Alex asked, already getting to his feet and placing an arm into his jacket.

"Take a statement from her. You might receive some backlash when you get there. At first, I told her we wouldn't be able to search for Carl as we're investigating the other cases. I went to pass it over to the desk sergeant but then realised the significance behind his disappearance."

"You think there's a link with the ongoing investigation?" Bob asked.

"Don't you? You know how much I detest working with coincidences. I don't think it would be right if we ignored this."

"I agree," Alex said.

He took the address from Sam, and he and Oliver left the room.

"Good luck," she called after them. She turned to find her partner staring at her. "What's that look for?"

"I didn't realise my face was any different than usual. It's called contemplation."

"Are you sure you don't mean constipation?"

The rest of the team laughed, and Sam chalked up yet another strike for herself, during what was turning out to be an intense investigation.

"Why do I bother?" he said in a huff. He folded his arms, and his head dipped.

Feeling guilty, she crossed the room and slapped him on the shoulder. "It was a joke."

"Do you see me laughing? I'm trying to be serious here."

She perched on the desk beside him and tapped the back of her hand. "There, I've reprimanded myself, how's that?"

"Like that counts. Anyway, do you want Liam and me to check the ANPRs for his car?"

"Yes, great idea. Holly said he was due to meet her for coffee in town today. Going by memory, I believe he lives above the pub, from the information Bethany gave me."

Bob nodded, and she left him and Liam to it. Claire raised her hand to gain Sam's attention.

"Have you found something else, Claire?"

"I did some research into Bethany's parents and discovered they both died in car accidents."

Sam frowned. "Accidents, as in plural?"

"Yes, the father was killed first, and within a couple of months her mother also died at roughly the same place, this time in a rented car. I suppose she was waiting for the insurance to pay out on the car, after it had been written off."

"Hmm... I've heard different accounts about her parents, none of them match those facts. Either this woman has had a very unlucky life or there is something far more sinister going on here than we first realised. What about her siblings, did you manage to trace any?"

"I did. It's not good news. Two babies, one boy, the other a girl, both died before they were six months."

"What? How?"

"Cot deaths, according to the death certificates."

"It doesn't ring true, or am I overthinking this?"

"No, I agree with you," Claire said.

Sam's gaze was automatically drawn to her partner who was pointing at the computer screen. She smiled at Claire, "Well done on what you've accomplished so far. All we need now is that damn warrant to come through. No idea why the dickens it should take so long for them to grant them these days."

"Same old excuse, Covid has a lot to answer for."

Sam nodded and wandered over to where Bob and Liam were sifting through the footage. "What are you getting excited about?"

"We've got an image of someone, dressed in the usual dark getup, lingering outside the pub this morning."

"Really? Let me see."

Bob angled the screen in her direction. At nine that morning, a dark vehicle with obscured numberplates entered the car park and slotted into a space at the rear, close to a silver BMW.

"I'm presuming that's Carl's car?"

"Correct. It was pretty easy for us to trace it. Here's Carl leaving the pub at five past nine. He walked towards the car, distracted, either viewing or sending a message on his phone. Here's the assailant, who whacks Carl over the head before he has a chance to look up from his phone."

Sam winced and gulped. "Poor sod, he didn't stand a chance."

She watched the assailant then drag Carl to the back of

the other vehicle and throw him in the boot which had popped open. "That car, can we identify the make at least?"

Liam glanced up at her. "I might be talking shite, but to me, it looks similar to the car that shunted you up the backside, boss."

Bob grunted and flopped back in his chair. "Fuck, you're right, Liam."

"Can you follow that car? Pick it up on the system? There should be a few cameras in that area, shouldn't there?"

"I can do my best," Liam replied.

"And what about the BMW, Carl's car?"

"We checked with the pub, it's still in the car park," Bob said.

"All very mysterious. What cars are registered to the farm?"

"I can double-check that."

"Do it. I sense we're getting close. Would you say the assailant was male or female?"

Bob nodded. "I was about to mention that. I think it's probably a woman."

"Listen up, everyone. I believe the great Bob Jones has finally come around to my way of thinking."

The team applauded, and Bob stood to take a bow.

"Seriously, we need that bloody warrant to be authorised. Maybe Bethany is holding both Jenny and Carl hostage in the farmhouse. Why else would she refuse us entry?"

"Possibly," Bob said. "Might be worth putting the farmhouse under surveillance until the permission comes through."

"Claire, chase it up for me. Tell them it's urgent. Enforce upon them that we believe several lives are at stake. That might shake them up a bit."

"On it now," Claire shouted back and picked up the phone.

Sam paced the floor, sensing they were getting close to solving the investigation, either that or it was about to come crashing down around their ears. The former would be preferable.

TWO HOURS LATER, Oliver and Alex returned with the statement from Holly, and they had finally received the news they'd been eager to hear all day, that the warrant had been granted.

Sam organised her team. Everyone, except for Claire, would descend on the farmhouse, along with several patrol cars.

The convoy of vehicles, six in total, drove out to the farm without the use of sirens or lights. When they arrived, Sam knocked on the door to the farmhouse, but it remained unanswered.

"Okay, Liam, you shoot round the back, see if she's in the garden. If not, we enter by force."

Liam shot off and returned a few minutes later. "No one there, boss. I peered through the kitchen window. It's a tip in there, but no sign of life from what I could tell."

"Let's do this."

The team stood back and allowed one of the burly uniformed officers to ram the door with the Enforcer. Once he'd battered it off its hinges, he stood aside. Sam and Liam withdrew their Tasers and were the first to enter the property.

Her nose wrinkled with the pungent smell, and she was forced to cup a hand over it. "Shit, the stench is horrendous. How could this place have deteriorated so much in just over a week?"

"Christ, and we thought the pigs had it rough," Bob said from behind her.

The team split up. A couple of uniformed officers, also carrying Tasers, searched the upstairs of the property, while Sam and the rest of her team continued to pick their way through the mess in the lounge, dining room and the kitchen.

"Anything?" Sam asked after their search had ended.

"Nothing. It's as though she's tipped every scrap of paperwork she's ever had to deal with in her life on the floor. Why?"

"My guess is she was searching for something in particular." Sam walked into the hallway. "Have you found anything up there, guys?"

"Nothing so far, ma'am."

Sam kicked her way through the mound of paperwork towards the table in the corner of the room, where they had initially spoken to Bethany and Jenny, when they had broken the news about Alvin's death, which seemed an awful long time ago. Sam pulled on a pair of nitrile gloves and sifted through what she presumed to be the more important sheets of paperwork. Underneath, she discovered a mobile phone. "It's an iPhone. Can anyone see a charger lying around?"

Oliver pushed the sofa away from the wall and found a charging lead in a socket behind it. "Here, boss. Want me to plug it in?"

"Yes, do it. I'm wondering if it's Jenny's. I'll give it a moment to come to life before I ring it."

When Liam gave her the all-clear, she removed her notebook from her pocket, flipped it open to Jenny's details and rang the number. The phone rang. Sam's gaze immediately sought out her partner.

He shrugged. His expression was one of remorse, and he mouthed an apology that she waved away.

"We need to search this farm from top to bottom. I want every available officer out here now."

Bob cleared his throat and said, "I'll get on to the station."

Sam kicked out at the paperwork littering the floor at her feet. "Where the fuck are you, Bethany Davidson? And what have you done with Jenny and Carl?"

"I need one of you to return to the station to check the CCTV footage. We need to know which vehicle she took and when she left the farm. I can't see her staying around here, can you?"

"I agree, boss. I'll go," Oliver volunteered.

"Thanks. Make Claire aware of the situation. We know there's only one road in and out of this area, so it shouldn't take you long to get a result."

"I'll let you know ASAP what I find, boss." Oliver left the farmhouse.

Sam moved over to the window and stared across the farmyard at the barn. Something in her gut was urging her to search the outbuilding.

Bob peered over her shoulder and asked, "What are you thinking?"

"There's more going on in that barn. The pigs were disturbed the other day. Yes, the sow had died, but what if something or someone caused the sow's death?"

"Shock! The beast might have died of fright, is that what you're suggesting?"

"I don't know, but something is drawing me to investigate the barn, thoroughly this time."

"I'm up for it, if you are."

Sam left the farmhouse at the speed of lightning. Her mind working itself into a frenzy, her thoughts travelling at twice the speed her feet were carrying her in her quest to get to the barn. She halted just outside the building and strained an ear. "That's strange. The number of times we've visited this place, I don't recall ever being confronted with complete silence, can you? Something doesn't ring true, not where livestock is concerned."

Bob shot ahead of her and pulled the door open.

"Fucking hell. It's a massacre."

Tears misted Sam's vision. "What the hell is going on here? These animals didn't deserve to suffer like this. What a fucking screwed-up bitch that woman must be. How can they possibly all be dead?"

Bob searched the immediate area and came up with the answer. "Over here, there's a hose pipe that's been shoved through the side panelling. It's got a rag around it to ensure air didn't get in. She's fucking gassed them, the lot of them."

Sam shook her head, sickened by the torture the animals must have gone through before their deaths. "This is too upsetting for words. Bob, ring the vet, get him out here. We need to check if she's killed any of the other animals on the farm."

Bob removed his notebook and dialled the number of the vet. Sam zoned out from his conversation and entered the pigsty She weaved her way through the dead carcasses to a mound of straw at the back that had drawn her attention. On the way, she glanced sideways to find that all the little piglets they had saved days before, had tragically also been slaughtered needlessly. Blocking out the image, she kicked away some of the straw. Only to jump back when a hand dropped out.

Sam slapped a hand over her mouth and let out a muffled scream. Bob swiftly appeared beside her, muttered a few choice expletives, then got down on his haunches and removed a clump of straw to reveal the face of the victim.

"What the...?" Sam whispered.

Greg Davidson's lifeless eyes stared back at her.

Bob stood and turned Sam away. "Don't look. And before you even go there, none of this is your fault. You warned him to stay away from this place. If he didn't heed your warning that's down to him, not you."

Sam covered her face with her hands. "Why, oh why, didn't I get the warrant sooner? All of this could have been avoided. Where are Jenny and Carl? I was half expecting it to be Carl. Never in my wildest dreams did I imagine it would be Greg."

"Me neither. Maybe he dropped his guard in her presence, and she took advantage of him when the opportunity came her way to do away with him."

"Jesus Christ. It's even more imperative we find her now, Bob. We can't allow her to get away with this. Shit! What else are we going to find?"

Bob gulped. "I dread to think. Something just crossed my mind."

"What's that?"

"The incident with the pigs. She didn't hang around, did she? Instead, she took off in that tractor of hers, under the pretence of feeding the animals in the top field. What if there was a body in the bucket and we spooked her by showing up when she least expected it? She was pretty quick to make her exit, wasn't she?"

Sam closed her eyes. "And what if it was Jenny and she disposed of her right under our noses? God, if that's the case, then I'm never going to be able to forgive myself."

"Stop it. I won't allow you to do that, Sam. If anyone is at fault around here, it's me. I should have supported you throughout the investigation instead of sticking up for and making excuses for the evil witch. I'm embarrassed that I allowed her to play me."

She offered up a weak smile. "We both screwed up. I need to get SOCO out here right away." She placed the call, all the while shaking her head in disbelief as Greg's eyes stared back at her. She knew that image would haunt her dreams for years to come.

After her call had ended, she retraced her steps out of the pen and stood by the door to rid herself of the toxins she had probably inhaled. "We need to get out of here, Bob."

"I'm right behind you. Do you need me?"

"What's on your mind?" Sam asked.

"I thought I'd take a ride up to the top field, see if there's anything up there that needs further investigation?"

"Go for it. Take Liam with you. Have you driven a tractor before?"

He winked at her. "No, but it's always been an ambition of mine."

"Wear gloves."

"Liam, over here," Bob shouted, almost deafening her.

Their colleague sprinted towards them. "Is something wrong?"

"All the pigs in the barn are dead, along with Greg Davidson."

"Shit, that's a shocker. What can I do to help?"

"Bob has volunteered to search another section of the farm, and I need you to go with him."

"Okay. Do I need to bring anything with me?"

"Have you got a shovel in the back of your car?" Sam asked, more out of hope than expectation.

"It doesn't matter, there's one leaning against the barn, I'll grab it," Bob said and darted off to retrieve the item.

"Put some gloves on," she instructed Liam. "I'll leave you two to it and go back in the farmhouse, have a root around in there until the vet arrives." Sam, her shoulders hunched, because of the weight of the world pressing down on them, returned to the farmhouse and began sifting through the paperwork on the table, ignoring the ones strewn across the floor of the lounge.

There were countless legal documents regarding the farm. No sign of a will, though, from what she could tell. She instructed the uniformed officers to wait outside the property until SOCO arrived. Deeming the paperwork irrelevant, she relocated and searched the bedrooms upstairs. She sought out Jenny's room first and checked her wardrobe and drawers. They appeared to be pretty full. Did that mean that Bethany had lied about the young woman packing a bag?

Too damn right she did. Every word that came out of her mouth was a bloody lie. She hoodwinked us into believing she was grieving the loss of her husband and all the while she was plotting her escape. But why kill Greg? Because he challenged her? Caught her off-guard by turning up at the farm when she least expected it? When she was in the throes of putting the final pieces of her plan into action? What a warped individual you are, Bethany Davidson. Fingers crossed we catch up with you before you get too far. What about Jenny and Carl? Where could they be?

Within fifteen minutes, the same vet, Nicholas Sparks, drew into the farmyard. Sam left the house and removed her gloves. He seemed subdued and demanded to see the animals. When she opened the barn door, he tried to walk inside, but she latched on to his arm.

"Sorry, I can't allow you to go any further, I need you to make an assessment from here."

"I'm confused. May I ask why?"

"Because it's a crime scene, and I'm waiting for SOCO to arrive."

"Since when are SOCO involved in a slaughtered animal ca…" He stopped talking and surveyed the area again.

"We discovered a dead body at the rear of the pen, in that mound of straw."

"Oh heck. Who is it? A member of the family? Were they killed alongside the pigs?"

"Yes and no. Yes, it's a family member, but not someone

who lived at the farm. I can't tell you anything else about it because that's really as much as I know. We found the body and put the call in straight away. I have no idea how the victim died, only that he was buried in the straw. I don't even know if he was either left to die or he was already dead when the pigs perished."

"And do you know how the pigs died?"

"Come with me." She led Nicholas around the side of the building and pointed at the hose pipe poking through the side of the barn.

"Are you telling me they were gassed?"

"So it would seem. The owner of the farm is on the run, and her stepdaughter is on the missing list. Our investigation has consisted of us sieving through numerous lies to obtain the truth. We're still none the wiser about things, not yet. I fear we won't discover what the truth is until we find Bethany Davidson."

He ran a hand through his short dark hair. "This whole situation has shocked me." He shuddered. "Why kill the pigs? Because she was intending to go on the run?"

"I can't answer that. Sorry to drop this bombshell on you, but I'm going to need you to check the condition of the rest of the animals on the farm. Can you do that for me?"

"Of course I can, it would be an honour. If they're alive, what happens next?"

Sam shrugged and held her palms up. "I really can't answer that. I was hoping you could work your magic with the community, ask them to lend a hand, for the sake of the animals, not to help out the woman who did this."

"I admit, the circumstances are somewhat different to when I sought help from the other farmers last time. Leave it with me. I'll assess the livestock for now and deal with the aftermath later."

Sam smiled. "I can't thank you enough for helping us."

The tractor rumbled past them.

"Sorry, I need to speak with my colleagues. Give me a shout if you have any further questions."

"I'll be sure to do that. I'm going to need to call the practice, get more bodies out here. This farm has over a hundred acres, I won't be able to cover it by myself."

She smiled. "Do what you need to do. If you can ensure the access is clear at all times, I'd appreciate it. There are going to be vehicles coming in and out of here all afternoon."

"Don't worry. I'll make the call."

Sam approached the tractor that Bob had switched off next to a nearby barn. He and Liam jumped down, their faces expressionless.

"Well, don't keep me in suspense, what did you find up there?"

Bob shrugged. "Nothing that was obvious. Maybe we're doing the woman an injustice and this time she had a legitimate reason for going up there."

Sam raised an eyebrow. "You carry on believing that, partner. I'm inclined to think otherwise, but like the vet has just highlighted, this farm has over a hundred acres for the techs to explore."

"Bloody hell, that's going to take forever and a day."

"Yep, tell me about it." Before Sam could say anything else, her mobile vibrated in her pocket. "I need to get this. The vet has called for assistance. We're still waiting for SOCO and the pathologist to get here, hopefully they're on the way by now." She answered the call. "Oliver, what have you got for me?"

"I've located a dark vehicle which I believe to be Davidson's, heading out towards Keswick, boss."

"I take it the numberplates are still missing?"

"That's correct."

"Okay, we need to put out an alert for the vehicle. We'll head over that way; I want to be there when she's arrested."

"Umm... there's something else you should know."

"Come on, Oliver, we haven't got time for this."

"There are two females in the car."

"Right! And?"

"And, from what I could tell, the passenger didn't seem to be in any kind of distress. Of course, I only caught a flash of them on the cameras, so I might be talking out of my arse."

"I see. Okay, thanks for the heads-up, Oliver. Keep in touch." She ended the call, and her gaze drifted back to the farmhouse.

"What's going on?" Bob asked.

Out of her peripheral vision, Sam saw his gaze flicking between Liam and her. "He's located the car on the way to Keswick, two females in the vehicle."

"Right, what else?"

"According to Oliver, the passenger didn't look distressed in the slightest. Have we got this all wrong? Are they both in on this?"

"We won't know the truth until we catch up with them," Bob said. "Not trying to tell you what to do, but have you thought about setting up a roadblock? There are far too many routes they can take around that area. It would be a nightmare scenario if we let them slip through our fingers now."

"Good shout. We need to get on the road. I'll drive, you make the calls. Hop in the back with us, Liam."

They ran towards the car as two vans entered the farmyard.

"Get the roadblock organised ASAP. I'll give Des the lowdown on what's happening." Sam jogged over to the pathologist's vehicle.

He was at the back, donning his protective suit.

"Sorry, I'm going to have to run through things quickly and shoot off." Which she did, while a stunned Des listened with a deadpan expression.

"What are you hanging around here for? Go, you need to get this twisted bitch off the streets and banged up."

"Thanks for understanding. The body is in that barn over there. There are dozens of slaughtered pigs in there, so tread carefully." She smiled and darted back to her car.

"All organised with the station. The teams are going to keep in touch with us en route," Bob informed her once she was strapped into her seat.

"Let's get this show on the road then, shall we, boys? I need to be there when the ground swallows her up. Her plan is about to backfire and blow up in her face. Hopefully we'll have a front-row seat to witness it."

As promised, the other officers kept them regularly updated throughout the journey. The closer they got to Keswick the faster the adrenaline pumped through her veins.

"I wonder what the rub is," Bob broke through the silence filling the car as the Keswick town centre sign emerged before them.

"You mean with Jenny?" she asked.

"Yeah. If, and it's a huge if, she's involved, I wonder what part she's played in all of this."

"Let's hold back on the speculations, for now, at least. Only because I'm finding that incredibly hard to believe."

"In other words, you need to see how the land lies with your own eyes first?"

"Totally. Don't you?"

"I suppose."

The call came through from the lead patrol car that

Bethany had put her foot down and was driving through the town centre like a woman possessed.

"Shit, she's the type not to be bothered about how many lives she puts at risk. Does anyone know their way around Keswick? Maybe we can take another route and cut them off."

"I know this area pretty well," Liam said from the back seat. "If you take a left at the top, that leads down to the river. Follow it for a while, and we should meet up with them at the end of that stretch of road."

"Brilliant. I'm glad you're with us, Liam, neither Bob nor I would have had a clue."

Sam resisted the temptation to use her siren as the roads were reasonably clear at this time of the year. She suspected, had the chase taken place in the height of the summer, they wouldn't have stood a chance of finding the suspect.

Liam's pointed finger shot through the seats between her and Bob. "There, that looks like them."

"You're right. Okay, here we go. Hold tight!"

Bethany's car hurtled towards them, followed by three speeding patrol cars.

"She's not slowing down. Prepare for impact, I refuse to let her get away from us."

"Jesus, you can't do that," Bob complained.

Sam yanked on the handbrake, and the car slid to a halt in front of Bethany. She slammed on the brakes, meaning the impact to the passenger side of the car was minimal in the end.

"Jesus, thank fuck for that," Bob shouted.

Sam tore out of the car. Liam had his Taser drawn and aimed at Bethany. Bob joined them after he'd crawled over the front seats.

Sam wrenched open the driver's door and grabbed Bethany's coat by the collar. "Get out. Bethany Davidson, I'm arresting you for the murder of Alvin Davidson, Mike Bartlett and Greg Davidson…"

"What? You killed Greg?" Jenny shouted from the passenger's seat.

Judging by her reaction, doubts flooded Sam's mind whether Jenny knew about the crimes or not.

Bethany grinned and tipped her head back. "It took you long enough to figure things out, Inspector."

"Not really. I had your card marked the minute I laid eyes on you. It was a matter of biding my time, waiting for the evidence to surface. You were sloppy, that was your downfall in the end."

"Whatever. You can talk the talk, Inspector. Let's see how you handle me at the station."

Sam grinned at her and then faced the two uniformed officers who had joined her. "I've never been one to turn down a challenge. Make sure she has a comfortable journey, gents."

"Don't worry, we will. What about the passenger, ma'am?"

"Slap some cuffs on her, too, I'm undecided about her part in all of this."

"What?" Jenny objected from her seat. "I'm innocent. She's held me captive for days."

Sam took a closer look at Jenny's hands and noticed the nylon tie around her wrists. "Okay, Jenny, I need to be cautious for now. Go with the officers, and you'll get your chance to share your side of the story back at the station."

Tears ran down the young woman's cheeks, and she shook her head. "Why won't you believe me? I could never kill anyone, let alone my own brother and father. I swear I'm innocent."

Bethany laughed as one of the officers placed a hand over her head and put her in the back seat of the patrol car.

Sam stood back, allowing a constable to assist Jenny out

of the car and watched as he marched her back to his vehicle, her wrists still secured by the tie.

"What are your thoughts about Jenny now?" Bob muttered beside her.

"I'm on the fence. If she was involved, why would her hands be tied? Saying that, it would have been easy for her to have inserted her hands in the tie during the chase."

"Yeah, I'm unsure, too. We need to see how the interviews go."

"Speaking of which, we should get back to the station." She held her hand up and deliberately high-fived Bob and Liam under the watchful gaze of Bethany and Jenny. Whether Jenny was a suspect or not, Sam sensed the rest of the day would be full of lies that would need to be sifted through to obtain the truth, unless they were both going down the "no comment" route. She suspected Bethany would, but Jenny remained an indeterminate proposition.

CHAPTER 10

Sam's intuition turned out to be correct, not for the first time during the investigation. Bethany remained tight-lipped and grinned malevolently at Sam throughout the interview. Sam had been determined not to waste too much time on the main suspect and decided the evidence they had discovered at the farm would end up speaking for itself, making it near impossible for Bethany to deny.

So, for the rest of the day, all her efforts remained with Jenny and the part she had played in the murders at her family home.

As soon as Sam and Bob entered the interview room, Jenny's tears bulged in her eyes. The duty solicitor, Miss Crane, had assured them that Jenny was innocent and had no part in the crimes.

Bob started the recording, and Sam fired her first question, her intention being to go for the jugular out of the starting blocks.

"Why did you get your brother involved?"

"I didn't, not intentionally."

"I only have your word for that, Jenny. You're going to need to be honest with me if you expect me to believe you're innocent."

"How am I supposed to do that? It's obvious you think badly of me. I swear, I had nothing to do with the murders. I only found out what Bethany was truly like when you showed up at the farm. I genuinely thought an outsider had killed my father and Mick."

"Did Bethany admit to you that she had killed your father and Mick?"

Jenny wrung her hands. "Not at first, but then she got annoyed by me moping about the house, in tears most of the time, and she blurted it out one day."

"When?"

"A few days ago. Up until then, she'd kept up the pretence. She caught me trying to escape out of my bedroom window at the end of last week and since then she's kept me confined to the house. When you visited, she shoved a rag in my mouth to prevent me from calling out for help. I was shocked when Greg came to the farm. She wouldn't let him in because I was in the lounge, tied up. You have to believe me, I had nothing to do with this."

"Has Bethany revealed why she killed your father?"

"No, but I figured it out for myself. It was because of the money."

"The life insurance policy your father took out a few years ago?"

"Yes. She was hoping the payout would come through quickly, didn't expect the insurance company to drag their feet."

"Why did she need the money so badly? Was she in debt? Did she think the only way out of her situation was to kill your father?"

"She never went into detail. Just told me that she intended to sell the farm and move to Cornwall."

"Why Cornwall?"

"She told me her heart belonged there. I don't know, I stopped listening to her sharing her hopes and dreams once I knew she'd killed my father. All I could think about was the pain and suffering he'd endured at her hands. I'm not just talking about his murder but also the years of manipulation that Dad and I had to put up with. She's never been an easy woman to live with. At first, maybe. But it didn't take her long to show her true colours. I would never have expected this from her, though. Not murder."

"Why didn't your father stand his ground with her? Tell her to change her ways or jog on?"

"Because he sincerely loved her and rarely saw the bad in people. When I tried to point out her failings, not only as a stepmother but as a human being, he refused to listen. Ended up taking her side, so the house remained peaceful. He was a lovely man, didn't have a confrontational bone in his body. And she was fully aware of it, had him wrapped around her little finger and was doing her darndest to get me kicked out of the house, but Dad was having none of it."

"So, rather than sit back and admit defeat in a losing battle, she went all out and ended his life."

"It looks like it. I couldn't have been more devastated when I heard he'd been killed. It never dawned on me that she was behind his death, not until Mick died and I sat back and thought things through."

"Why do you think she killed Mick?"

"I presume because he was very close to my father, and when he showed up for work, he had an attitude towards her that pissed her off."

"What about your ex-boyfriends?"

Jenny frowned and glanced at her solicitor then back at Sam. "I don't understand."

"Neither do I," Miss Crane replied. "Care to tell us where this line of questioning is leading, Inspector?"

"When we showed up at the farm yesterday, needing to speak with you, we were under the impression that you had gone missing. Bethany couldn't supply a list of your friends for us to contact, but she did give us the details of your three ex-boyfriends. Can you tell me why?"

Jenny shook her head. "No, not at all. I can't think of a reason, in fact, I'm shocked she could lay her hands on their details. She hated them, couldn't wait to see the back of them and even cheered when I admitted the relationships were over."

"I have news for you. One of the men, Carl Scott, has been reported missing by his current girlfriend. Do you know where he is? We have reason to believe that Bethany abducted him, but we don't know where she's taken him."

Jenny gasped and slapped a hand over her chest. "My God, no, I don't know anything about this."

"Are there any other barns where he's likely to be held at the farm?"

"There are the barns around the farmyard, but there's also a hay barn out in the fields at the rear of the farm. Dad erected it so he didn't have to keep dragging hay back to the farmyard. Might be worth trying that."

Sam nudged Bob. He took the hint and for the recording, excused himself from the room to make the call. He returned a few moments later and nodded, letting Sam know her instructions had been actioned.

"Where were you heading when we picked you up in Keswick?"

"I'm not sure. Bethany refused to tell me. I think she had Penrith in mind, she knows that area a little." Jenny's gaze dropped to the table. "I'm not convincing you that I'm not involved in this, am I?" Her head rose again, and she looked Sam in the eye.

"In all honesty, I truly don't know what to believe, Jenny. I don't feel you're reacting like someone who was abducted. A few tears don't wash with me."

"How am I supposed to act? Look at my nails, they're bitten down to the quick. They've not been that low since I was thirteen. If you want me to collapse into a heap, it's not going to happen, I'm not the type."

"I appreciate people deal with stressful situations such as this differently, but I wouldn't be doing my job properly if I let my guard down."

"Why won't you believe me? Because I was in the car with her? Would you have treated me differently if she had shoved me in the boot of the car? Is that what you're saying?"

Sam stared at her and nodded. "Perhaps."

Fresh tears dripped onto Jenny's cheeks, and she threw herself back in the chair. "This is so wrong."

"I agree," Miss Crane interjected. "I don't know what else my client can say to alter your opinion. Don't you think she's gone through enough in the past few days?"

Sam sighed. "Okay. I'll release Jenny, but only if she agrees to check in here, at the station, every day for the next week."

"Jenny, can you do that?" Miss Crane asked.

Her eyes widened, and she nodded enthusiastically. "Yes, please, I won't let you down. I don't know how else I can prove my innocence."

"Very well. Miss Davidson, you're free to go. I'll introduce you to the desk sergeant, he's the one you'll need to report to daily."

"I won't let you down," Jenny repeated.

EPILOGUE

Over the coming week, Sam spent a lot of the time up at the farm. Jenny was a willing participant in the search for her ex-boyfriend, Carl. His body was eventually found in one of the fields; one of the techs decided a fresh mound of earth needed further investigation. Jenny was beside herself, and when the news was broken to Holly, Carl's current girlfriend, Jenny volunteered to comfort her, but Sam had advised against doing that, especially when it was obvious that Bethany had killed him and tried to dispose of the body. The main lingering question Sam had about Carl, was why Bethany had bumped him off. But then, nothing should surprise her where that woman was concerned. As others had said, she had evil running through her, and in Sam's vast experience, people with a warped mentality rarely thought logically about anything.

Recapping the notes Bob had taken down during the initial interview they'd held with Bethany at the farmhouse, one piece of information lodged itself in Sam's head that she had trouble shifting. Bethany had told them that Alvin's brother, Stuart, had tragically died whilst working at the farm, and Bethany had also let it slip that she was the one driving the tractor that had killed him. Was that truly an accident, or had the intent to kill him off been there all along?

Sam had run her theory past DCI Armstrong, and he had shaken his head.

"I wouldn't bring that into the equation, Sam. His wife has put it in the past and probably got on with her life by now. There will be very little evidence to back up your theory anyway."

"Little evidence?" Sam had replied incredulously. "She's a serial killer. That's all the proof we'd need to put yet another nail in her coffin, surely."

He had shrugged. "My advice would be to leave well alone."

"I can't do that, sir. At least let me run it past the CPS, see what their take is on it."

"Very well. But don't let this information get out, let's keep it between you and me and the CPS, for his family's sake."

"If you insist."

That conversation had been held a few days ago now, and her contact at the CPS had agreed with Sam, much to Armstrong's dismay. The outcome of which was that Sam now had to visit Stuart's widow to share the news of their suspicions, but that could wait for twenty-four hours.

Now, she had an important family issue that needed her immediate attention. Crystal was at her father's house. She had phoned Sam, telling her that he wasn't in a good way.

Sam dismissed the team and headed over to her father's. Despite trying to prepare herself en route, she hadn't anticipated how bad he would be.

Crystal greeted her at the door.

"How is he?" Sam asked. She removed her coat and hung it on the hook in the hallway.

"He's not good. You'll see for yourself. I'm worried about him."

Sam hugged her sister, and they both inhaled a large breath then fixed a smile on their faces before they entered the lounge. Sam's gaze was immediately drawn to the mess littering the floor surrounding her father's chair.

She cleared a space, kissed him on the forehead and knelt beside him. "Hello, Dad. How are you?"

He stared at her, his eyes glassy and watery. "I wish I knew," he muttered.

"What's going on? Can you tell us if you're in any pain, Dad?"

Her father clenched his fists a few times and then lifted his left hand to cover his heart. "Yes, here."

A lump formed in Sam's throat. "Oh, Dad. We all feel her loss, it'll get easier with time. I promise you."

"Don't give me that bullshit. This pain will never leave me. Look around you, I'm surrounded by memories of her. They're there when I get up in the morning until I close my eyes at night, if I ever do. Sleep, ha, what's that?"

Sam took his hands in her own. "Dad, it sounds to me like you need grief counselling. One of us will go with you if you need us to."

"I don't. No one will understand what I'm going through. How do you get on with your life when you've spent so many years with such a special person? I thought I would feel her presence... I haven't, not once since she left me. We made a pact that we would always be there for each other, visit the other one when we passed over. Why hasn't she kept her promise? What did I do wrong?"

Sam cleared her throat and glanced sideways; Crystal was wiping the tears from her eyes.

"Dad, we need to give her time to settle into her new surroundings. Knowing Mum, she's probably up there now, catching up with all the folks we've lost over the years."

"Either that or she'll be bossing people around." Crystal laughed which brought a smile to their father's face.

"Now that I can believe, except she would call it *organising* those around her, she was an expert at doing it."

Sam touched her father's face. "That's the spirit, Dad, think of all the good times you had together. The pain will ease, I promise you. Look, if ever you get down, just give either one of us a call. We've both offered you a spare room for the weekend or a day during the week if you need it."

"I know, but the last thing I want to do is become a burden to you both, you have your own lives to lead."

"Nonsense, you're still an important part of our lives. We'll get through this together. You need to do your part and push the anger at losing her to the side."

"It's easier said than done, love."

Sam kissed him, and the three of them shared a group hug.

"We're here, supporting you if you need it. We love you, Dad."

"I love you, too. My world would be a very lonely place without my two beautiful daughters to support me."

The tears flowed, and they didn't stop for a while…

"We love you, Mum," Sam whispered.

THE END

THANK you for reading To Believe The Truth the next thrilling adventure is **To Blame Them**

Have you read any of my other fast paced crime thrillers

yet? Why not try the first book in the DI Sara Ramsey series No Right to Kill

Or grab the first book in the bestselling, award-winning, Justice series here, Cruel Justice.

Or the first book in the spin-off Justice Again series, Gone In Seconds.

Perhaps you'd prefer to try one of my other police procedural series, the DI Kayli Bright series which begins with The Missing Children.

Or maybe you'd enjoy the DI Sally Parker series set in Norfolk, Wrong Place.

Or my gritty police procedural starring DI Nelson set in Manchester, Torn Apart.

Or maybe you'd like to try one of my successful psychological thrillers She's Gone, I KNOW THE TRUTH or Shattered Lives.

TO KEEP IN TOUCH WITH M A COMLEY

Pick up a FREE novella by signing up to my newsletter today.
https://BookHip.com/WBRTGW

BookBub
www.bookbub.com/authors/m-a-comley

Blog

http://melcomley.blogspot.com

Why not join my special Facebook group to take part in monthly giveaways.

Readers' Group